Magdalena Tulli

MOVING PARTS

Translated from the Polish by Bill Johnston

archipelago books

Archipelago Books
25 Jay Street #203
Brooklyn, NY 11201
www.archipelagobooks.org

Library of Congress Cataloging-in-Publication Data
Tulli, Magdalena.
[Tryby. English]
Moving parts / by Magdalena Tulli ;
translated from the Polish by Bill Johnston. – 1st ed.
p.cm.
ISBN: 0-9763950-0-2
I. Johnston, Bill. II. Title.
PG7179.U45T7913 2005
891.8'538 – dc22   2005016693

Distributed by Consortium Book Sales and Distribution
1045 Westgate Drive
St. Paul, MN 55114
www.cbsd.com

Jacket art: *Self-Portrait: The Constructor,* El Lissitzky, 1924
© 2005 Artists Rights Society (ARS), New York / VG Bild-Kunst

*This publication was made possible with support from
Lannan Foundation and with public funds from the
New York State Council on the Arts, a state agency.*

NYSCA

*This publication has been subsidized by Instytut Ksiazki –
the © POLAND Translation Program.*

Moving Parts

THE CREATION OF WORLDS! NOTHING COULD BE SIMPLER. Apparently they can be conjured out of thin air. And for what? To delight the eye with their shimmer as they ascend toward the light, trembling like soap bubbles. Then they're swallowed up by darkness. When they rise, it's as if they were already falling. But are they not splendid? They're casually called into being and thrown carelessly into the void; there is no one to save them. The narrator, a rather secondary figure, knows nothing more about it; he acknowledges this with regret. Alone and faced with accomplished facts, he is concerned about one thing only: that he should avoid descending into banality from the very first sentence. If he could, he'd prefer to walk away with his hands in his pockets, leaving everything to the mercy of fate, which he has not been permitted to influence; or at the very least to abide stubbornly in an eloquent, arrogant silence. But the narrator realizes he has nowhere to go. The privilege of arrogance is also denied him. The kind of life that has fallen to his lot, insofar as it can even be called a life, offers no opportunity for choice. A tale someone has nonchalantly conjured up must suffice for the entire substance of his existence. A tale hungry for subjects and predicates, lodged in their tissue like a rare species of rapacious parasite. The narrator would dearly like to believe that the one who summoned him into being knows more, that he comprehends the whole and knows the ending. But the latter does not appear in person either on the present page or those following; he doesn't respond to letters and faxes. It may be that for weeks he has been languishing in bed, in rumpled sheets, turned away from the world, face to the wall, surrounded by empty bottles or used needles; who could possibly know? So when a tragic turn of events elicits giggles from the back rows, or when a joke dies in cheerless silence, the narrator knows that there is no one he can turn to, and that the whole affair is his responsibility alone. He must button his lip in humility, then move on to the next sentence as if nothing had happened – like a clown in checkered pants who, falling off a chair amid peals of laughter from the audience, immediately starts to climb a rickety stepladder without interrupting his monologue: a pathetic figure, peremptorily consigned to a here below comprising a ring yellow with sawdust, tripping up again and again on even ground, and trapped in perpetuity in the vicious circle of the show. The acts likely to appear in the sawdust-strewn ring are tediously familiar to all those sitting in the rows of seats, including the small children, who fidget as they wait for the performing elephant to make its entrance. The monologues too are known by heart, including the round button of the last sentence on which the loop of the beginning is fastened, and also the dubious, unconvincing conclusion, which induces no more than a shrug of the shoulders. Every word has been heard a thousand times or more. What does it matter that it was in other sentences? No one is interested in the details. It's all so numbingly hackneyed, say the glazed looks. This is precisely why it's better to be a reader than a narrator. It's pleasant to chew gum, set the rustling pages in rapid motion and, when the last one is turned, to toss the book back on the shelf. This is a better fate than losing one's pants in foolish pursuit of a runaway story line entangled in the breakneck acrobatics of tightrope walkers and the tricks of conjurers, and to end up being struck on the nose by a slimy apple core flung by some unknown hand. There, in the middle of the ring, under the gaze of several hundred pairs of eyes, almost anything can happen and nothing will surprise anyone – it's just that it's best not to wipe one's face with the large polka-dot handkerchief, the same one that barely a moment ago served as a prop. It's more advisable to bow low over and over, with a broad red smile painted on one's cheeks, and – without sparing one's arm – to sweep a battered bowler hat back and forth in the air. Scarcely having reached a place where a period can be inserted, the narrator already begins to question whether a circus farce can bear the weight of what was to be conveyed here. Maybe the weary audience staring at the ring would pay only enough attention to the external world to understand every bow in an utterly literal manner. If the narrator's voice strives too insistently to draw attention to itself, it will call forth an angry impatience; a humble request for a handout would be more favorably regarded. And thus there is no chance of a conspiratorial wink, no whisper of solidarity. Nor any hope of avoiding solitude. But while we're on the topic of comparisons, isn't it better to be a narrator than a character? Who would want to be a character, walking on a tightrope strung between a lost past and an uncertain future, like an acrobat in a close-fitting leotard that shows the working of his musculature and his vulnerable abdomen, numb with fear? And all this is still too little; in a short while the audience will fall asleep from boredom, unless the acrobat gets a partner, her skimpy costume glittering with silver sequins, a huge pair of butterfly wings adorning the shoulders. If she is as reckless as he, she'll fling herself into his arms over the abyss, trusting him blindly, out of necessity – or possibly counting on the safety net, if one is in place. But it is only without a net that the show can be truly enthralling. The vast space overhead takes one's breath away, and for a moment it seems to the spectators that it's their own bodies teetering on the ropes up above, where no limitations can be seen, and where freedom, one would think, is in plentiful supply – that they themselves meet there and separate, and pass each other over the void, and that the space belongs to them.

Either way, separation is unavoidable: The acrobat faces a triple somersault with a landing on the bar of the trapeze, though this may be too much in light of the offhand tone of his contract, in which everything essential is expressed in a sparing and matter-of-fact fashion with the aid of a handful of figures. And not a word is said about the mortal danger to which one of the parties is exposed by rashly appending his signature. What he is throwing on the scales is a priceless possession that cannot be recovered in case of loss. Even his life insurance policy, a document of dubious utility whose very title impresses with facile promises, will be of no use in such a case. Alas, the acrobat has learned only how to balance over the abyss; he has no other skills, and so he does his job while his partner plunges into the void. Sparkling with sequins, in a rustle of butterfly wings she plummets head first, as if she were no longer needed in the act. But her appearance isn't over yet: Just in time she reaches through the air and grasps the bar swinging upward in a broad arc, and once again she shoots overhead, soaring into space. If she doesn't break her neck, they'll meet on the trembling platform under the slightly faded canvas dome of the heavens, and from there they'll slide down into the center of the ring, all of a sudden, as if they'd landed from the moon. He'll put his arm round her waist, they'll bow right and left, and the band will play a flourish.

They stay in decent hotels. At a table covered with a snow-white cloth they blotch their morning papers with fragrant coffee and spread butter on their rolls. Before anything happens to them, for a good beginning they have the discreet clink of silverware and the sound of car horns entering from outside. The melodies of cell phones ring out one over the other. The noises of the early morning are chaotic but promising, like a cloud of tones of open strings in which can be heard chance snatches of a concert not yet begun, taken up now here, now there, quickly and without expression, in ironic summary, from the orchestra as they tune their instruments. And almost everything seems possible when the evening is still so far away.

They are in no hurry; they sit with their elbows resting on the edge of the crumb-strewn table. The woman, in blue jeans, takes a cigarette from a packet lying on the table. The man gives her a light; his biceps bulge beneath his black sweater. They talk. What can they be talking about? She laughs, looking directly into his narrowed eyes; she tilts back her head with its short red hair, blows out a cloud of smoke and taps ash into the ashtray. If she wished to act like a woman sitting at a table in a hotel dining room with a man in a black sweater, there is nothing more she would have to do. While they remain at the table they look happy; a thoroughly secure future extends before them: in the morning coffee and rolls, in the evening somersaults over the abyss, and so on for all eternity. Is this enough to make them feel confined by the circus metaphor in which their fate is enclosed? And even if so, do they have any course of action other than to take up the life that has been assigned them in this tale? Perhaps it would be better for them to remain forever at the table set for breakfast, she with a cigarette, he with coffee cup in hand, and between them on the white tablecloth, let's say, a green apple, which somehow neither of them feels like eating. They'd sit like this endlessly, sprawling on padded chairs whose softness comes from the pink stuffing hidden under the upholstery. It isn't difficult to imagine what hardships, mortifications, and disappointments these two would be spared. But no one wishes to remain forever in an inconsequential moment. Thoughts flee from it in reverse gear toward accomplished facts, while desires, having nothing to look for in the past, rush forward at breakneck speed. Only the second hand of a watch thrashes about in the present tense, trembling nervously. All alone, over and again it passes by the two broader hands as they turn unhurriedly in their matching orbits, evidently connected with it only mechanically. The rhythm of its feverish twitching is foreign to them. To the body though it is only too familiar – the delicate body, warm with desires, which, surging toward the future, at that very moment collapses into the past, sinking helplessly into it, enmired. And while the moment called the present still continues, its existence is felt merely as an uncontrolled turmoil of heart and mind, a chaos from which one tries to flee as far as possible. And so the dining room will soon empty and the pair finishing their breakfast will eventually vacate their chairs, abandoning green apple peelings and the crumbs scattered over the tablecloth. Are those their cups, with a mouthful of coffee left at the bottom, traveling away on a nickel-plated cart? They merely passed through their hands, amid the clatter of silverware and the murmur of voices forming the daily loop between the dishwasher and the table. The man is seen again briefly in the lobby behind the glass pane, then the woman too; in the background there are large sofas, in whose insides pink stuffing covers the unpleasant steel spirals of invisible springs and gives the leather upholstery a rounded appearance. We'll learn that as they were drinking their coffee, their suitcases, ready for departure, were waiting by the front desk, at the crossing of ways that lead to train stations and airports – where all worlds meet and where any character is expected only to complete certain uncomplicated formalities. The last of these will be to wish a toneless good day, which must be acknowledged a moment before the final parting in a damp and dark early morning in, let's say, November. One's gaze has to glide over a glass jar filled with candies that no one takes. With the bill in one's wallet, one disappears in the twinkling of an eye, not leaving behind an empty space, nor a hint of longing, nor a breath of regret. The nature of suitcases is such that they are both there and not there at the same time; the gleaming floor already shines through their substance, and it will remain in its place once the cases have gone off in the trunks of taxicabs. On the other side of the mirror-smooth slabs of synthetic stone to which mud will not cling, let us imagine at least two floors of cellars, with plumbing, central heating pipes, a series of transformers and coils of cables. And still lower a bottomless chasm, the same one in which southern seas bristling with coral reefs mortally perilous for sailing ships, and roiling with waves of unassuaged emotions, extend all the way to the lifeless northern seas sheeted with permanent ice, their frozen waves covered with hoarfrost. In the antipodes of the present world of the hotel lobby where every object stands in its place, one can expect a realm dispossessed of all order in which top is bottom and down is up. The sofas, armchairs, and tables of that other world, deprived of solid ground, fall chaotically, directly into the void of that reversed sky, into oblivion. Tablecloths slip from tables and sail through the air, crumpling and folding; plates and silverware fly every which way; tea splashes from teapots. Everything comprehensible and obvious here, in that place must appear tortuous, indecipherable, absurd. But the flooring of synthetic stone conceals the dark gulf, persistently imposing itself on the eyes; one's gaze slides involuntarily across the reflecting surface. The pair to whom so much attention has been paid has called not one but two cabs. Each of them will now depart in a different direction. The man in the black sweater slips the hotel receipt into his wallet; in his eyes is repeated the row of lamps shining coldly over the counter. The short, simple surname the receipt is made out to may begin with the letter M. And that is the last that's seen of them. The tale is like a hotel; characters appear and disappear.

The narrator feels tired at the mere thought of the next sentence, though the story hasn't even begun. It could be thought that all this time it has been spinning its wheels, emitting a hum thoroughly reminiscent of street sounds muffled by panes of glass. Its emptiness and sterility are written in the dull-colored plaster and the indifferent sky. One feels like ordering a beer and watching the foam settle in the mug, nothing more. If the narrator could choose, he'd prefer to tell about things free of complications, about leather-bound furniture exuding the cool tranquility of affluence and fortunate never to feel the weight it is its lot to carry; about glistening tiles of synthetic stone; about spotless panes of glass; about white porcelain cups in sets of six dozen – if one or two are broken it won't be the end of the world. If the narrator really could choose, he would prefer not to tell about anything at all. Then where did this next character come from? How could he suddenly have come into view? He has arrived in a taxicab that drove around a square on which a bronze horse covered in green patina rears on its hind legs bearing a rider encased in armor. A few sparrows have taken wing from the raised visor. The newcomer has paid for his ride and is climbing out of the cab. From his pocket there juts a folded newspaper; it could, for example, be the Financial Times. This vignette is an agreed-upon signal intended especially for the narrator – a sign that forces itself on his gaze.

Let's say that it is still raining. Let lights be reflected in the wet asphalt as if it were a mirror; let clouds pass across the puddles, and in the aquaria of the shop windows let umbrellas rise, weightless as jellyfish. The raindrops have already added a spotted design to the plain fabric of the man's jacket. Let's say that his overcoat was stolen at the airport. Did he also lose his wallet, tucked into an inside pocket? The wet sidewalk reflected the lights of the hotel, while the semitransparent image of the bronze rider shook slightly in the glass of the revolving door and spun on his horse as if on a merry-go-round when the new character entered the lobby. Across the mirrors drifted the aforementioned jacket, an immaculate white shirt collar and a necktie that is rather ironic, but also rather flashy – of course, within the limits of what's permissible in places where the only salvation is to reconcile freedom with servitude. Narrators have a fondness for details; they pluck them skillfully and with relish out of the background. The necktie tells them almost everything, while the eyeglasses merely reflect the external world, little more than a fragment of a setting that narrators know like the back of their hand. Different profiles and faces are chosen for jackets than for black sweaters; foreheads can be smoother, gazes milder, and this principle, let it be noted, has been upheld. Despite this, it's hard not to notice a striking resemblance between the two male figures, especially when the strip of lamps shining coldly over the front desk flashes in the newcomer's glasses. The reservation is found under the name of a well-known shipping company whose shares have for some time been considered an excellent investment. Having the traveler's expert knowledge at its disposal, the firm did not omit to arrange for a roof over his head, forbearingly, with resignation even, accepting the fact that he, too, has a body, as troublesome and demanding as any other. On the hurriedly completed form there briefly appeared a long and illegible name beginning with the letter F. The top-class specialist, whose involvement guarantees success for the company – by now it's certain that it is him – reaches for his keys. The tan lines on his hand reveal that as recently as July or August he was wearing a wedding band. He could have taken it off a quarter of an hour ago even, slipping it into the same pocket from which the now unnecessary newspaper protrudes. But the smiling desk clerk doesn't fall for such a trick – neither she nor anyone else. In the meantime the bell of the elevator rings out over the door with its steely gleam, described in the trimmings catalogs as a half-matte easy on the eye. The door opens and closes with a barely audible hiss, easy on the ear, and F. is already exiting on some floor or other; thick carpeting muffles his steps. He opens the room vacated by the other two, which by now has been cleaned so thoroughly that no trace of them is left. F. ought immediately to put in a call to his bank and give them the numbers of his lost credit cards. Instead, he rakes his fingers through his hair and goes up to the window. So it's possible that his wallet remained safely in the inside pocket of his jacket, though even in this matter there can be no certainty, for there exist states of mind in the face of which the security of one's bank accounts is of no importance. Mr. F. stares at the dull plasterwork and the gray sky that the narrator was reluctant to observe. He, too, has no wish to look at it; he draws the drapes carefully. He isn't missing much. Walls and clouds were, in any case, blocking the view. There was no way to see beyond what was in plain sight. F. sits on the sofa, then lies down on it, like a passenger on a ship who has been overcome by the nauseating pitch of the vessel and has retired to his cabin. And thus a maritime metaphor encroaches on a foaming wave between the lines, thwarting the earlier circus metaphor that the narrator had only just finished dealing with. The new complication perplexes him. From the slipshod, woefully incomplete score with which he was provided, an equally important second subject is emerging. The rhythm is familiar – that of cautious steps over the abyss; in it one senses the quivering of ropes strung between the masts of a circus tent, or a sailing ship. This rather unexpected response to the first subject, which was presented in the passage containing the circus fanfares, is introduced, let's say, by the French horn – does it not roar out in the voice of a ship's foghorn? Either way, the second subject has now been imposed on the narrator without a trace of decency or sympathy, since in the parts of the score that are supposed to give a sense of the whole, gaps have been left. It isn't clear whether the one who appointed the narrator left him without guidelines through an oversight, or whether perhaps he neglected the details, preoccupied with some other, more important task. Or he simply couldn't be bothered, and so deliberately shirked the effort of finding harmonies. In place of a round island yellow with sawdust and washed by lofty waves of admiration and awe, from the heights of the crow's nest there can be seen somewhere down below the deck of a sailing ship tossing on the ocean waves. The planks of the deck have the same yellow color of untreated wood; the clamorous undulations of the audience closely resemble the sound of high seas. In essence we are still dealing with the same thing: that which is visible. Then what is the essence of the invisible structure, its foundation and its core? Maybe the ropes strung across the abyss; maybe the ocean currents in the depths; maybe the precipitous lines of the graphs of market reports in the columns of the Financial Times. F. cannot know this either, since others who are better informed also do not know. No handbook can resolve the matter; no trade journal will figure it out. F.'s hand falls limply to the floor, as if he were asleep, when suddenly a sob issues from his throat. This sob will be heard a floor above by the maid when she turns off her vacuum cleaner for a moment. Is this really the room left by the other two? There's no doubt about it; never mind the details. Whichever of the numerous rooms on many floors it might be, it would always be the same one. His other hand pulls the tie over his head, reaches for his collar and loosens it with a single tug, ripping the button off. In this scene the pop marks the turning point, which has just passed. From this moment all is preordained, with no return and no escape. It transpires that the well-paid professional with the ironic glint in his eyeglasses who was seen only a moment ago in the lobby and at the front desk – does not exist. The character lying tieless on a hotel sofa is not to blame for this. The fault lies with the troubles of life, with the dull plaster, the gray sky. It lies with hope or with the lack of hope – there's no difference, since hope and lack of hope both lead to the same point.

The narrator could assert that he saw with his own eyes the events that took place in the hotel lobby, and likewise the arrival of the cab. He watched them through the glass panes, over a beer, which at his request had been brought to him in the dining room, even though the tables were already being cleared after breakfast. But how was it with the interior of that room on some floor or other? This is a critical question, assuming the world actually exists, and does so reliably enough that we should not consider ourselves entitled to discuss uncertainties. And could the narrator drink his beer if the world didn't exist? But in fact he didn't drink it at all. He merely watched the foam settling in the mug.

There now reappears the question of the rolls that the other two spread with butter not so long ago: it would be nice to know for certain that they at least actually existed. The narrator smirks when the word 'actually' moves full sail into the dangerous straits that have emerged between the image of the rolls and the period. In order to eat the rolls one must have a body – it's as simple as that. Body and rolls are of the same substance. There's no need whatsoever to concern oneself with what that substance is; it's enough that there is someone to name the one and the other – and thus the narrator pulls out of his ear an egg that he had only just put in his pocket, and takes a bow. The body is indifferent to this entire matter. Naive and simple-hearted, it wants only to experience good; it desires nothing but comforts and pleasures, and that is why sofas sink so softly and caressingly beneath its weight, and why cream is served with coffee. On the other hand, that which is called life demands impossible positions of the body. It requires monkeylike agility for climbing masts; it requires crawling on one's knees with a scrubbing brush across the planks of the deck, in gleaming white dress shirts, in jackets on which there is not to be a single speck of dust, nor drop of brine. What torture it is to sail day after day in the fog of the present tense. Subjects and predicates welter in it devoid of outlines, drifting without goal or direction. Until they are stopped by a period at the end of a sentence, everything still seems possible; every unexpected "therefore" opens the sluice gates to seas of subordinate clauses, to narrows of ironic meanings, to foreign ports of perverse conclusions in which the last word casts doubt on the first, like a customs official boarding a ship at the end of its voyage and looking for any pretext to question the bills of lading and discreetly pocket a wad of crumpled banknotes. The fog lights of adverbs and complements summon one fragment after another from the hazy background; let's look for instance at a bright smudge of red moving through the grayness of an autumn afternoon. It's a red umbrella, which a fourth character is just about to fold with a snap. The narrator hopes that at this point he'll finally be able to put his foot on the dry land of the past tense, in the kingdom of certainty where facts live and flourish. Only there do they flourish, nowhere else; the past tense is their entire world, the homeland of truths that are incontrovertible though, it must be admitted, usually contradictory.

Up until now the narrator has been given no opportunity to speak with someone in authority who would have a better idea where this story is heading; and so the course of events takes him by surprise time after time. Having no binding agreement to rely on, he had wished that three characters would be the end of it, but it was not in his power to insist. And so the figure with the umbrella is crossing a damp terrace covered with dead leaves. It's still the same November. Somewhere in the corner, garden furniture has been stacked in a soggy pyramid. The torpor of autumn has deprived its forms of lightness. Raindrops tremble on the upturned backs of chairs; the fancy cast-iron legs jut skyward. The season is over, and nothing more will happen; as for the next one, no one knows if it will ever come. The whole property is for sale, and has already been assigned a number in the listings of the real estate agency; the description is accompanied by a photograph in which the succulent green of the trees stands out against a cream-colored façade. Under the heading 'garden' is frozen the mute echo of bursts of laughter at a table adorned with red wine stains and lambent patches of sunlight filtering through the glass tableware. By the gate next to the bell push a metal nameplate of no use to anyone has been put up; never mind what it says. The narrator will ignore the first letter of the surname; he's already grown tired of the game involving initials. When the key grates in the lock, an empty interior will open wide to reveal white walls and ceilings; a staircase will lend the space depth. Rectangular marks on the wall are mementos of frames that must have held pictures; but of what? The punctured remains of a colored rubber ball will be lying in the corner beneath the stairs, until the sale of the house summons new owners; but this is foreordained, and so the floor will seem to show through the rubber integument. The lighter things are, the easier it is for them to disappear, as if they were blown away by a gust of wind produced by the difference in air pressure between future and past tenses; in recesses they last longer. It would seem that when buying, for instance, such a solid thing as a grand piano, one could count on its weightiness, on the boundless durability of its black lacquer, and on the immutable laws of harmony. But it was placed, as sometimes happens, in a draft, and so the piano passages, volatile shoals of triads that cannot entirely be taken seriously, died away first, before the murmur of voices, and even before the smell of coffee had dissipated. The perfection of a silence capable of containing all sounds will no longer soothe any ear. The furniture has vanished, along with a colorful mist in which life was pleasant and imposed no thoughts about its direction or its meaning. Even the umbrella stand has gone, and so water drips onto the floor, onto the perfectly maintained beechwood tiling, while the female figure turns in her hands an envelope taken a few moments ago from the mailbox. It can be surmised that the trick involving the juggling of passions worked perfectly for her for a very long time; the golden balls of love, jealousy, and longing, obedient in her hands, passed through the emptiness of the spheres as they described their giddy, collision-free double and triple trajectories high over the depths of despair, far from the misery of ruination, leaving no trace other than streaks of light. Ink can stain; a mark has been imprinted on her index finger. It's a capital F. from the last name of the addressee, turned back to front. Stubborn, it managed after all to find a way to appear. The first letter of the sender's name, also smudged from the dampness, tries to squeeze into the next sentence, but without success. The forwardness of these capital letters has gone too far, thinks the narrator. In any case the woman still tears the envelope into shreds, along with its contents. Now she needs to get rid of the pieces and doesn't know what to do with them; she ought to throw them into the toilet and flush them away. After all, she must know where the bathroom is. While she's at it she ought to put the red umbrella in the bathtub. But whatever she does now, it will not satisfy the narrator, who has already allowed the insidious word 'ought' to take control, peremptorily imposing its weight on the sentences. And thus, because of the last name beginning with F, probably her husband's, out of wifely loyalty she ought to stick to the metaphor of life as a sea voyage, and especially avoid the circus images associated with the character in the black sweater. Either way, little here depends on the opinions expressed by the narrator. All he can do, and that only to a certain degree, is to govern grammatical forms, an essential element, especially as concerns the verbs, which are constantly striving to escape into open space, of their own accord taking on the forms of the future tense, without any obligations. Brought forcibly down to earth, while they still can they steer clear of perfective forms; they thrash like kites and drift toward waters into which one cannot step twice, and even at a distance it's evident that as the lesser of two evils they prefer to spin in the eddies of the present.

In the narrator's view the future tense doesn't give facts the necessary grounding. It's as shapeless as clouds in the sky, and if it brings any order whatsoever it is only an ephemeral and unimportant kind. On the periphery of the landscape the clouds assume new forms, tattered and swirling, and they are illuminated all of a sudden or, on the contrary, darken in shadow. In this way the feathery clouds of summer evenings have been transformed into storm clouds creeping ponderously across a leaden sky on dark bellies that bleed purple from their lacerated sides amid fireworks and the rumble of drumrolls, in the cascades of a downpour. Water is the only thing they are capable of turning into when floating through the sky eventually becomes impossible: a process as violent as the transformation of future into present. After the repertoire of special effects is exhausted, the storm clouds sail on in the guise of night clouds, black against a black background, invisible. In the end, even if weeks later, they manifest themselves as white billows against a white backdrop, equally invisible, bringing an image of nothingness from which the female owner of the still-conjectured piano turns away with repugnance. The early dusk falls quietly, without the extravagant splendor of the after-glows that, for instance, during the preceding summer flamed over the garden every evening, lighting up the charming little wisps of pink fluff scattered here and there over the horizon – the same material that lends softness to padded furniture and plush toys. The same that eases sorrow, providing warmth and smoothing the merciless hardness of edges. Without which life would not be possible. It hovers high up, light, elusive. In the heavens there is nothing but transient states, nothing that can be taken into possession.

The dry land so longed for, the solid ground of the past tense on which the foot can find support, unfortunately contains much more than necessary. It's filled with the leftovers of other similar tales, and the fading dreams and desires of figures who are absent and irretrievably lost, mixed with the shallow sand of all the parts of speech. In the darkness of the subsoil the suns of past summer afternoons are extinguished; transitory romances crumble into dust. Eternal love gravitates toward deeper levels of ground, where it grows damp and bereft of luster, like a tarnished wedding band. Along with it molders spurned love. The heavy layers of earth crushing it can be regarded as a metaphor for a memory incapable of forgiveness.

If a spade were to sink into this soil, the blade would make a rasping sound, so riddled is it with the petrified word 'why,' a question without an answer, and so filled with shards of shattered and forgotten conditional constructions. How much of this debris could lie in the rectangle of the garden, surrounded by its chain-link fence? No one will take the trouble to count rocks that are of no value whatsoever. It's hard to say which one comes from which structure and what story it belongs to – this one or another – for unasked questions always take on the same indefinite shape, always the same murky shade of regret. If only they could be dug up and disposed of by the ruthless, tried and tested method of the mercenary corn cartels, whose brokers are constantly monitoring the changing prices in the tables of the commodities markets, and thanks to the amazing new capabilities of wireless telegraphy can manage market swings, in an emergency ordering the crews of steamers to throw burlap sacks of wheat into the ocean without a second thought. The sky in its indifference remains discreet; all around there is nothing but water, impatient and rippling. The voracious sea fish are already waiting, ready to gnaw through the burlap and swallow any amount of grain. But even they will not touch rocks. Meanwhile, in the depths the tireless ocean currents sweep up everything that lies in their path and cast it on land many sea miles, many calendar years away.

And what if one were to begin to fence off the stories, just for the sake of order, so it might be known which one begins and ends where, and who it belongs to? One thing is for certain: The soil inside and out, on our side and on the other, would be equally rocky. Such an operation too would be pointless: For worms and moles a fence is no obstacle, while hobos can vault over it when no one's watching. Clouds at least, once set loose, float off wherever the wind drives them and don't come back, which unfortunately cannot be said of the questions buried in the barren sands of stories. The very thought of their monotonous drifting evokes tedium. The narrator cannot see a good way out for himself, since the actual way out – the stylish revolving glass door beneath the gleaming inscription – is not meant for him. The freedom with which hobos jump over fences stirs a longing for open spaces in the narrator. The hobo, who in the meantime has taken shelter from the rain under a torn shopping bag, casts an indifferent glance at the letters over the entrance, which form into a name, let's say, Universum. Any name is as good as any other, so long as it contains sufficient luster to gild the letters. And indeed, though they can't be seen from inside the lobby, in this case one can be sure they're gold. The narrator imagines that if he could, he'd set off without hesitation on the trail of the faded army surplus jacket that is presently growing wetter on the hobo's back. Where would it lead him by the end of the day? How far to the east, west, north, or south, how deeply into the clefts of the past tense? The hobo stares through the panes of glass at the cigarette butts in the ashtrays; he'd clearly like to light up, but he doesn't have anything to smoke: The butts from the sidewalk are presently swimming in puddles. In his ear there glitters an earring, a reminder of a better past life and a conventional sign of freedom. Yet freedom has its limits, inflexible as a sheet of glass, though just as invisible. The glass doorway is not meant for the hobo, and so he'll stare for a while and move on. By chance he is passed by an elderly gentleman, a retiree perhaps, with a small boy. The tramp, always prepared for rejection and accustomed to receiving it without anger, might have accosted him and asked for a cigarette, but he abandons the idea in time. A refusal would have been inevitable, because the boy is wiping tears from his cheeks and wailing in despair. The elderly gentleman is growing impatient. He's dragging the boy along behind him and carrying an umbrella, and in addition he has to bear his own body. This body, tormented by shortness of breath, sinks under its own weight. From time to time his old rheumatism, a reminder of certain damp trenches, makes itself felt in his knee or his shoulder. The past weighs the most; it fills the body like a boulder. But the body ought not to complain; it is neither hungry nor cold. It's dressed in good-quality gray woolens, and everything the body might find useful has been placed solicitously in the pockets in advance: disposable paper tissues, a comb, mint pastilles in a small tin. Nevertheless, the body is filled with resentment: It demands the respect owed to age and the weight of the past, and it especially insists on consideration for those immemorial trenches, which here are thoroughly irrelevant. The elderly gentleman in gray woolens believes that the commonplace tale of his long life is here a leading theme of the greatest importance, while in reality this tired body will always be floating on the fringes of the actual story, occupying only episodes. There's no lack of stories. They're all over the place; thanks to unlimited supplies, they can be had for a song in any quantity. Yet no one wants them; the narrator also would rather steer clear of them. If in spite of this an episode such as the present one captures his attention, it's only because of certain additional possibilities concealed within it. If these possibilities are given a say, they'll inescapably alter the course of all subsequent events, at least to the end of the paragraph. The boy will break away from the elderly gentleman and will run into the roadway, right in front of an approaching van. The vehicle will brake with a squeal of tires. Two men in blue overalls will jump out. One of them carries the photograph of a little girl in his wallet. The girl and the boy are the same age and look very much alike, but for obvious reasons this is hardly the moment to be showing pictures. The elderly gentleman finds no response to the angry gestures of the man in overalls; he merely shakes the boy without mercy. The umbrella trembles in his other hand, while rain drips down their necks. But now this is of no significance to the narrator; the van is already in place – where it was meant to be, expressive and indispensable as a chord closing an overture.

It has stopped, then, in front of the hotel, one wheel riding up onto the sidewalk. In it are long flat styrofoam packages. And for sure also a toolbox. Sets of handy screwdrivers are carried in the pockets of the blue overalls. The two men take them out and set about removing the revolving door. In the required sequence they unfasten everything attached with screws and everything clipped into place. The bronze armor first, then the horse's head, then the forelegs and hind legs. And all the events that have flashed past the hotel door with the monument in the background now equally become subject to dismantlement. Strips of paper are soaked by the rain; the wind blows scraps of styrofoam along the sidewalk. Four axleless panels stand for a moment in the lobby alongside four new ones, which glisten just the same, almost indistinguishable. And now the men in overalls have finished the job; they set in motion that which they have taken from the factory packaging and assembled into a new whole. They've done this dozens of times. They hang on the handrails and turn in a circle, checking that the mechanism works as it should. In the panes of glass, instead of the rider and horse, a fountain is reflected. A fountain that stands in the middle of the square in place of the monument. Its bronze bowl is covered by the same green patina. For a moment it looks as though the narrator will manage to escape into a different story. Things are better this way.

Or rather they could have been better, but someone was evidently against it. And so the narrator is obliged to begin a paragraph in which the desk clerk's cry will ring out and be broken off suddenly, breathless, at its highest point. Shortly, in the background will be heard the wailing of police sirens and ambulances, first in the distance, then closer and closer. It will prove necessary to mention the portable posts between which plastic tape bearing official diagonal stripes is strung, closing off part of the sidewalk around the entrance; also the crowd gathered behind this makeshift barrier, and the civilian officials of the investigation team picking their way through broken glass. And since all these circumstances have been brought up, it won't be possible to steer clear of what is most important: a series of shots from an automatic pistol that brought down the two workmen in their blue overalls as they were trapped between the panels of the revolving door. They fell where they stood; only their hands slid down the glass lingeringly, as if in slow motion. Their fingers grasped helplessly at the sharp edges of the bullet holes, leaving disquieting red streaks – an image that is disagreeable and also in its literalness somewhat ridiculous. And all this amid office buildings where work goes on in a frenzy of boredom and routine from morning to night only so as to have money; the more that's earned, the broader the scope for desires, which are uncomplicated and quickly fizzle out. The image is blurred; a misty suspension of rain falls slowly, enveloping the adverbs of time, place, manner, and purpose in every sentence. No meaning can be discerned in this image, especially if the evening newspapers suggest that the shots missed their presumed target. Accustomed to descriptions of paid murders, readers of the press will surmise the existence of a hired killer who was most probably shooting at a speeding car. The bullets are said to have found their victims at random, which ought not to surprise anyone. It's all the same to the world who happens to be in the line of fire, one person or another; which person is which is a matter of indifference to it. In certain circumstances a knight can perish at the hands of a bishop or vice versa; but the difference between them in essence will remain unclear and doubtful, explainable only in terms of movement and direction. The latter, as everyone knows, moves diagonally across the whole board, so long as nothing stands in its way, while the former dodges, attacking the other pieces surreptitiously out of the blue. Yet it can't be understood why one is one and the other the other, which authority decided it would be so and why; they could just as well have decreed that from now on the opposite will be the case. And since a complete reversal of roles changes nothing, it's all the easier to comprehend that it makes no difference to the bullets either. Afterwards, staring at the corpses, the onlookers succumb to the illusion that the inertia of death is a perfect match for precisely this body lying forlornly on the sidewalk, and so in the end they walk away reassured. Violent scenes always have their complement; after the culmination of tension the crowds pour into movie theaters, stores, and cafés humming with idle conversation about pleasant trivialities. And finally there comes the moment of relaxation that everyone deserves, when the tape and the official posts are no longer needed, the shards of glass all swept away, and in the immaculate panes of glass the rider and the rearing horse beneath him rotate again as if on a merry-go-round.

Looking behind the paragraphs for a path leading beyond what is visible, the narrator has found only confusion. Behind the paragraphs things are the same as everywhere else, only in disarray: broken glass, jumbled sounds. So let's gaze at the raindrops striking the windowpane – now they are in the foreground. There's no escape, and it may be necessary until further notice to move amid pieces of scenery set up ahead of time in between which not even the slightest gap can be discerned. Wherever one looks there are walls, floors, and ceilings, earth and sky. Scattered here and there is the sadness of unfulfilled desires and the sadness of desires fulfilled, each equally opaque. There's always something that a sensitive body wants and something it doesn't want, and it yields just as easily to euphoria as to despair. Since nothing can be done for it, at the very least it avoids protruding edges and is cautious when handling knives. The defenseless skin solicitously conceals some secret truth: a greedy stomach, delicate intestines, a few liters of blood that can be discharged in the blink of an eye, spilling beyond recall – and above all, the incessantly beating heart, which may never know peace till it bursts. In such conditions the charming little flowers on the meadows of bedding fabrics lend the pillow an ironic quality. But the body, trustful and yearning for sleep, is unaware of this. As for the white batiste that simply cries out for lace, it only seems not to impose its own essence on bedrooms: Whiteness is at root a provocation, and lace impresses with an ephemeral innocence about which it can be said merely that sooner or later it may be soiled, and it's easy to imagine pillows trampled by heavy boots, lying in mud, perhaps stained with blood. But the body refuses to hear anything about this. Nor does it wish to know about the blindness of bullets, nor the cold gleam of a steel barrel, nor the plump worms that live somewhere down in the earth.

One might now expect a question asking who this narrator in fact is, unabashedly permitting himself conclusions of this kind. Whether he also has a body to bear, whether he has feelings and desires, and what gender he is. The attempt to determine gender in particular is always reasonable. Here there are only two possibilities for defining all beings, with or without a body. The narrator is a man; he cannot be anything else. This is imposed by grammatical forms, especially those of the verb, though of course they are not the only things that follow so naturally after the word 'narrator' – pronouns should also be mentioned. Their testimony is consistent, and therefore irrefutable. It's not enough to say that they reveal the truth, since in fact they create it. The narrator knows that grammatical forms submit to his will only reluctantly, to a degree limited by their own routine way of manifesting themselves; moreover he can never be certain that it isn't they who are making use of him. The scrap of existence that fell to his lot should not exclude the possibility of experiencing feelings, though these kinds of feelings don't have to be – and why should they? – the slightest bit nobler than is generally accepted. All he can do is remain to the end hidden behind the screen of the third-person style, which protects his feelings from idle curiosity arising from boredom. The passing moments stir emotions in him like a current of water stirring a muddy riverbed. They leave behind a turbid deposit, a trace of longing. It is promise and hope that turn into longing, a sign that the moment has already gone – weightless, incorporeal, possible only as a parting without farewell. White tablecloths, the aroma of coffee, a stray shaft of sunlight in a glass of beer bring temporary consolation, but they cannot assuage the longing.

And the four characters of this story – at least one too many – shouldn't count on anything more as they wander through the murky space. Wasn't this supposed to have been a short tale of betrayal pinned on a three-sided frame? The fewer the characters, the simpler the narrator's task. He could still pretend that he has forgotten about the desk clerk, and ignore her existence the way he ignores the leather armchairs in the hotel lobby. But all that was needed was a moment of distraction, the confusion that arose as he was gazing at the smooth and clear panes of glass, seeking a good way out for himself, for additional, redundant figures to appear; they've already dispersed among the walls, among the furniture, considerably more than the four which should have been consented to at once, like it or not. Moreover, the narrator may be sure that if any one of them is overlooked, gaps will emerge and the story will stop running smoothly. It's too late now to get rid of the hobo with the earring, the retired gentleman with rheumatism, or the little boy. And also the workmen in overalls, even if appearances suggest that from where they were sent by an unfortunate combination of circumstances, they will no longer return. They can't be expected to content themselves with the gentle presence granted to those who are dead and are reconciled with death, free of resentments or hidden intentions, their silence concealing nothing. Even less can a courteous passivity be counted on from the alleged paid killer, and there is no hope that he at least, lurking unseen, can be excluded from the subsequent course of events.

Every turn of affairs has its price, enforced as relentlessly as the prices of goods placed on a slowly moving belt at the checkout counter of a store. Not even a fiasco is free. And in fact it costs the most of all. The thrifty customers compare price tags with cool calculation, figuring out how much they can afford and denying themselves one thing or another. And it's only when they are thoroughly embroiled in the ups and downs of their stories that their heads start to spin, their reason is impaired and they choose courses of action for which they lack the wherewithal. If the balance sheet is to add up, someone else will have to pay. And best of all would be if that someone just disappeared from view immediately afterward. No one wants to be in debt. Are narrators made of a different clay than everyone else? They would wait in vain for gratitude and compassion, and thus they themselves are also essentially ungrateful and feel no compassion for anyone.

Such comments prefer the muddy waters of the present tense; they wallow in them, especially if they're unwilling to enter into details and merely wish in their slapdash way to grasp the essence of things. And so no end is in sight for the torments of associating with the present tense. Its waves, now descending into the clownish rhythm of generalizations, now bearing like dirty foam the words 'probably' and 'let's say,' wash over the clauses of complex sentences, one after another, immersing them in uncertainty and ignorance. The narrator remains calm, having nothing to lose in the surging waters. Only the scrap of life that is his lot, and the unpleasant burden of an imposed duty. The present moment is a hotbed of confusion through which one treads without seeing a thing. The hand and the head float separately in it. Shoes appear alternately to the rhythm of the steps, now the right, now the left. And one may feel more or less as if between head and feet there was absolutely nothing except the roiling depths. The present tense commands life and death, but it is plagued by indistinct outlines, undulating shapes, and hazy backgrounds, and so the decrees of fate are capricious and blind. Of course, the metaphor of the waters has its limitations, like everything. The narrator's clothing has not absorbed its moisture; nor do his shoes, never mind what make they are, leave wet footprints. Though he does wear shoes. This doesn't mean that he bought them in a store, that for example he sat on the little measuring chair, that for him boxes were taken down from the shelves and opened and he was shown successive choices until at last he decided on a pair. Nothing of the sort – he was called into being complete with shoes, and now they are stepping softly across the middle of the lobby. In a moment they'll go down some narrow stairs. The iron structure twisting in a spiral might surprise an eye that had previously admired the interior of the lobby, glittering with gaudy newness. But in any case it's out of sight, well hidden from the gaze of guests lounging in the leather armchairs. These are old walls; what is new are only the panes of glass and the slabs of synthetic stone, so smooth that the sediment of memories doesn't settle on them. Was mention not already made of levels of cellars in which one can walk along passageways amid a tangle of piping and cables? And why should one walk there at all? Why should one then take another staircase, wooden this time, over which there hovers the musty smell of turpentine floor polish? A burgundy carpet, fixed to the steps with blackened brass rods, muffles the sound of footfalls. The somewhat timeworn paneling has taken on the dark hue of mahogany in the light of bracket lamps with chiffon shades reminiscent of the days of narrow-waisted dresses for women, and for men the opposite – loose-fitting jackets with padded shoulders and wide pants with cuffs. Nothing else should be expected in the oldest wing of the hotel, given over in its entirety for the use of permanent residents.

The narrator calmly opens and closes a double door and puts a bunch of keys on a round side table. He was given a room with a balcony and is living in it, whatever that might mean. From the height of several stories he sees miniature cars of all different colors moving along the roadway. Higher up are rows of roofs, chimneys, billows of white steam issuing from ventilation shafts. Clouds drift over the rooftops, one after another. Every kind of cloud, though – it goes without saying – never at the same time. It would be a simple thing to calculate how many of them have floated by since the hotel was built until the present moment. But this doesn't mean that the narrator has watched every one. He was summoned to being along with the window outside which all these clouds have passed, along with the snows that fell from them and melted, along with the rains of former seasons. With a whole prior life, so that it doesn't look as though he were born yesterday. Apart from the dull clouds over colorless and rumpled November mornings when everything seems unimportant, there also exist fluffy ones, white as ice cream on hot summer afternoons, that stand wide open toward long, warm, brightly colored evenings; and also little luminous clouds that pass like falling petals across a wasted spring afternoon a moment before dusk. Yet the unease that prevents one from staring too long at a darkened sky must have a cause. To be safe, it would be better to block the door with a heavy armchair. Then the distance from the balcony to the chair is no greater than ten paces; the narrator crosses it unhurriedly and at the armchair turns back. When he's once again at the halfway point there is a knock at the door. This moment is best endured in immobility. The knock may repeat; it may repeat many times. For a moment it may turn into a thunderous hammering. Is it really necessary to go into such details as the dust rising from the door frame? That which is pushed by the hands of a watch weighs nothing at all; in the end silence falls, as if there were no one on either side of the door. Silence is the natural state to which any noise must return, and from a certain point of view, on each side of the door there is in fact nobody, and the narrator ought to confess that he is aware of this. Nevertheless, a moment later receding steps are heard on the creaking stairs. It's only now that it is possible to look calmly at the blue of denim overalls passing through the gloom in a blotch with hazy edges in ever lower regions of the field of vision – which is extremely narrow, restricted by the sides of the keyhole – and eventually disappearing without trace below its bottom rim. The narrator is not curious to know what the figures wanted from him: extra attention, special privileges, an opportunity to finally remove the little girl's photograph from the wallet, an action for which suitable conditions were not created on the previous occasion. As if the photograph were supposed to lend support to predictable complaints and claims, above which there still rises the pathetic question 'why,' and even worse, the importunate word 'let,' the latter paving the way for a frontal attack by exclamation points with excessive demands. The narrator, barricaded inside, attempts just in case to ignore the ringing telephone, too. But, tormented by its insistence, in the end he reaches for the receiver. What happens next is not as hopeless as might have been expected. A polite female voice passes on a message concerning the actions he needs immediately to undertake; that's all. Instead of a guiding principle that would give his labors a meaning, he has to be satisfied with the promise of payment to be made in the afternoon. The instructions assume tacitly that any kind of doubt yields before the irresistible power of money.

Determined to do his job at the lowest possible cost, the narrator sighs and sets to. From the drawer of the nightstand he takes out some scraps of paper covered in handwriting. The writing is smudged and the text illegible. Water has dissolved the glue; nevertheless, out of the fragments with their torn edges it's possible to assemble the shape of an envelope, like a jigsaw puzzle. Stamp and franks in the upper right-hand corner. And so it's only an envelope. The letter is missing. The narrator never saw it. Addresses contribute little; the substance that was to move the story forward is lacking. Disappointed and angry, he pushes the torn pieces of paper aside. Yet one way or another he has been provided with nothing else, so he must reach for them again. Excessive damp has washed away the shapes of the letters; a magnifying glass merely enlarges their ambiguity. It lingers on the misshapen splotch of the letter F beginning the surname of the addressee, then moves over the short name of the sender, from the capital M to the point where it disappears in confusion and indistinctness beneath the imprint of a wet finger. One can be sure now that the addressee and the sender will appear again, willfully running rampant amid the scenery. Just a moment ago the narrator was counting on the story fading away of its own accord, like a lightbulb cut off from the electricity, or a car engine deprived of gasoline. But the stubborn letters M and F have achieved their end and have dragged the plot toward themselves; now there is no hope they will give up easily. The initials will not suffice, for they cannot be declined grammatically, and without this it won't be possible to keep up with the characters. And so the narrator tries to decipher the rest of the sender's name, the one that begins with M. It would probably have been simpler to read it from the circus posters, on which all the letters maintain their places in a row like trained animals. But the narrator hasn't seen these posters either. And so he tries to make it out: Is it Mozhe, or Mozhet? The name looks to have been hauled from some out-of-the-way corner of Eastern Europe, from the sign-board of some pharmacy, barber shop, or grocer's that hasn't existed for a hundred years. Could the first homeland of these couple of syllables have been the Cyrillic script? The ending of the addressee's name is much more clearly preserved. Accustomed for generations to the angularity of Gothic script, it can easily be imagined on the moss-covered headstones of a Protestant cemetery down a country lane. But the middle part can no longer be deciphered; at least the envelope will be of no help in this regard. The first names have become no more than ink blots; the shape of one of them recalls a circus tent, while the other looks more like a ship. The one thing that at this point seems more or less certain is that Mozhet's and F-meier's ancestors in their day shot at one another, trapped in damp trenches, the same ones that for peace of mind the narrator would rather pass over in silence. Unshaven and exhausted, they remained at their posts, living on hardtack and jam. Then their time came to an end, and all was for nothing. All the same it is not entirely out of the question that F-meier and Mozhet, who are as alike as two peas in a pod, are by a curious coincidence related. Blood becomes mixed beyond the broken front lines, when soldiers seek a woman's warmth. After all, an argument against kinship cannot be the anonymous bullet that one of those ancestors fired almost a hundred years ago, and that may have struck the body of the other.

The narrator reaches for the bunch of keys now lying on the

round side table. One of them will unlock a narrow door in the corner of the room that might have led to a bathroom, but in fact opens onto a dingy landing. Here, sure enough, the faded image of a gentleman appears on a further door, behind which one can be certain of a cracked urinal, white tiles and age-old cobwebs hanging from the ceiling; and opposite the door with the sign, a wire grille conceals the shaft of a freight elevator. Let us leave unspoken the inevitable question of whether the narrator avails himself of the urinal. A thick layer of dust covers all the surfaces; numerous tracks of the narrator's shoes indicate that he has stood on the landing before, and has even paced back and forth across it. The elevator arrives squeaking and juddering and slowly comes to a halt with a deafening clatter. It's enough to open the metal door with its cracked glass pane and take a step forward, and one is standing in the rickety cage. In the dim light of a dirty electric bulb a button can be chosen from which the number of the floor has worn right off. Now the elevator begins to descend, and along with it the sentence in which it appeared, and the next, and the one after that. If this handful of sentences were tied together with a decent length of rope, suspended from a pulley and lowered many floors down, from the narrator's point of view the result would be the same. In the end he leaves the cage of the freight elevator, slamming the metal door behind him. He knows what to do in the darkness that surrounds him. Flicking on his cigarette lighter, he finds the light switch – and everything immediately resumes its place in the cold, quivering glow of neon lighting: forking passageways, their walls, ceilings, and floors. The walls are plastered in a slapdash manner, the ceilings low, the floors hidden beneath a dense coating of dust, which here and there has turned into mud. In places there are even puddles; drops of rust-colored water hang over them from the joints between pipes: When one drop falls, another instantly takes its place. The narrator looks unsurely down the different passageways, though in fact he has nothing to think about: Both floor and course are imposed upon him. Naturally, various routes are possible, given the innumerable combinations of floors and directions, which cause the heads of clueless narrators to spin. Those who are more worldly-wise realize that of all possible paths there is always only one that is accessible; the others are closed, and the bunch of keys rattling in one's pocket most certainly does not include any that would open their locks. So nothing remains but to walk down the passageway before the automatic light switch turns off. At the end of the passageway the narrator will pass a pile of red fire extinguishers, no doubt past their expiration date, and with a long key he'll open a room filled with old copies of the Financial Times piled high against sloping walls – this must be an attic. He won't tarry there a moment longer than is needed to open a trapdoor in the floor. He climbs down a decrepit ladder and stumbles over a rubber ball lying in his way. The ball rolls down the stairs to the first floor, out onto the terrace and into the garden, with high, light bounces. From the top of the staircase it will be visible through a window, a patch of color against the grass. Through the window the narrator will see the central point of his story and its entire gold, green, and blue luster, focused in one happy place – a brightness that did not suffice for the less privileged days of the year, for the passageways moldering in shadow and confined between bars, for cramped recesses where colors darken with the same everyday grayness. The garden, then, in the middle of a warm summer. A green lawn and a sunny terrace beneath a blue sky. The air has been growing hotter since morning; in it the yellow blooms in the flower beds seem to glow with their own light till nightfall, when it grows completely dark, though only while the summer heat wave continues. Then their time comes to an end. This is the only flaw in the dazzling scenery. F-meier appears as its owner. His wedding ring still gleams on his finger. He leans against a garden chair, in a light-colored linen jacket that he can wear to work during the few short weeks of summer. He is smiling, but already looking at his watch; he's just about to drive off in the car standing in the driveway. Mozhet or Mozhe, in a striped sailor T-shirt, is taking more coffee. He has no office he must go to; the morning belongs to him, today and every day, and this gives him an unimaginable advantage over F-meier. So he exercises his privileges while he still can. On one of the evenings mentioned in his contract it may suddenly transpire that he paid for them dearly. The time, clearly, is too early for a visit; Mozhet's clothes are rather homely. It's easy to figure out that he has been staying in the guest room upstairs. Nothing can be heard, yet certain words are said. They accompany the look that the woman exchanges with F-meier over the table. Her hair is dyed red; the highlights catch the sun. Smiling, she exchanges the same look with Mozhet; more words are uttered. Never mind the words – it's obvious that nothing here depends on them. F-meier takes a packet of cigarettes from the table and looks around for his lighter, which the woman – his wife – finds under a newspaper. She throws it to him, and he catches it deftly in midair, puts it in his pocket and gives a bow of acknowledgment with which his slightly ironic necktie is in perfect harmony.

This time, so far the narrator has managed to limit things to three characters. The acrobat's partner is absent, though she knows this scene in the sunny garden; she's seen it many times in the movies, the same one or something similar. She knows how it could have come about and what is still to happen in the best or the worst case. Let's say that right now she is sitting in the dentist's chair, her mouth wide open, her jaw numb and beads of sweat on her forehead. The whirr of the drill leaves no doubt: If anesthetic has not been administered, it's going to hurt. It's even possible to imagine tears running down her cheeks; the reason seems understandable and the dentist would have to know a little more to guess that the problem lies rather with the patient's heart. And yet there is nothing to cry about; those three people, too, are only dreaming of the summer's day.

They're dreaming that they are sitting in the garden; they're dreaming of a romance. How can they possibly have a romance when they haven't even been given a real life? It could be said that they do not have the garden either, the green, nor the blue, nor the gold luster. And even if it were all actually taking place – what on earth could the acrobat do in such a garden for the whole morning? Perhaps he could carry the rubber ball around on his head, or walk about on his hands, whistling; or in case of necessity, he could even swallow burning matches and breathe fire like a dragon. That cannot have been what he came for. But the boy would have been enthralled. Probably. Had the car not come to an abrupt stop, with a squeal of brakes, before reaching the main road. Turning around, it races back at breakneck speed, as if F-meier, who is behind the wheel, had suddenly gone mad. Almost smashing into the gatepost, he leaves the key in the ignition and the driver's door open. As he walks, with an impatient gesture he takes off his glasses, which may have misted over. He's already back on the terrace; he puts the glasses on the edge of the table and says something to Mozhet, but what? The latter slowly raises his startled eyes at him and stands hesitantly from his chair; he seems a little taller than the other man. F-meier's tie is awry; its jokey pattern no longer matches the scene. He punches the other man in the face. Now the woman turns and casts a quick glance at the window of the room where the boy is in bed. The previous evening, for a long time he was unable to get to sleep; he cried and moaned. It's certain that several stitches will be needed over the eyebrow, though the tightrope walker seems not to realize it. Blood streams over his eye and cheek. It's already stained his striped T-shirt; he's smeared it across the back of his hand and has even managed to dirty the tablecloth as he reached for a packet of disposable tissues. He opens the packet clumsily and tries to wipe the blood from his face, as if unaware that the situation is serious and requires surgical intervention. Wads of bloodied tissue multiply. Mozhet doesn't know what to do with them; they fall at his feet one by one. He has not looked back at F-meier once. He gazes only at her, through one eye, because he can no longer see through the other. Half a look must now suffice for a farewell. He takes a step back, and his chair overturns behind him. He wants nothing, not even his leather traveling bag, it seems, which is standing on the floor in the guest room somewhere upstairs. From the first phone booth he finds, he'll call a cab; evidently he has his wallet with him. He's on his way to the gate when the woman pushes F-meier away from her, simply tears herself free; perhaps there is a shout, but it cannot be heard. She gets into the car abandoned on the driveway and burning with a metallic glare in the blinding sunlight; she picks up the man in the striped T-shirt and takes him to the hospital, and that's all. Meanwhile the tightrope walker's blood soils the light-colored leather upholstery of the car. And yet it is F-meier, her husband, who has gone mad and needs help. He sits motionless on the terrace, his forehead resting heavily on the edge of the table, not knowing how he will live through the next quarter of an hour. It would be better if the boy were not to wake up now. A soft breeze begins to rustle the newspapers scattered about the table. They include, let's say, the German edition of the Financial Times and an illustrated weekly with a well-known title, also German. Or perhaps Austrian? The narrator does not know; he doesn't read the German-language press, and in fact does not know German at all. Then what was the language of the spoken parts, which in any case could not be heard?

It couldn't have been German, of course. It's easiest to imagine that all the dialogues are conducted in the language of the narrator, not that of the characters. This is a method familiar from the movies; it enables the audience to understand a plot taking place in exotic countries, whose very existence is not entirely beyond doubt. Like it or not, then, the characters speak a language with flexible word order, in which anything can be said at least ten different ways, with different nuances of meaning. A language that suffers from an insufficiency of past and future tenses and a lack of rigor in their sequencing, something that permits the verbs a considerable degree of license and can lead to unexpected turns of events. This tongue, living happily under the aegis of Latin letters modified in makeshift fashion, has occupied a blank space on the map and has marked it with geographical names that everyone has heard of. Yet the fact that they are widely known does not alter the conviction that in essence Germany borders with Russia and Russia with

Germany – and that on one side of the frontier there lies dirty snow, while on the other colorful butterflies flit about. That's right, on both sides Polish is spoken. There is no other possibility. And in the Balkans? Polish too. And in the ports of the Far East. And in the remotest corners of Africa. Only Polish. Everywhere.

This still isn't the end of this scene, which, as it happens, is of crucial importance, and which the narrator, finding no other way out, had to come upon one way or another. While he's about it, he would gladly read the previously ignored name-plate by the gate, but he's reluctant to cross the terrace while one of the characters remains at the table. It would be less awkward to find amid the floors and passages the right hallway leading to the empty house and the abandoned November garden. But why doesn't F-meier call a cab and go where he is urgently needed and seriously late? Why has he still not found a babysitter for the child? The phone rings. A mouthful of orange juice from the bottom of a glass gurgles in his dry throat. F-meier is choking. The phone gives a second ring. It was her glass. Another mouthful, this time from Mozhet's glass – he, too, had left his juice unfinished. How can he now produce a voice from his throat? F-meier doesn't know, nor does the narrator. The third ring sounds sharp and insistent. The cordless phone is lost somewhere among the newspapers. F-meier finally answers; from the entire chaos of the moment the appropriate words suddenly leap out and arrange themselves in the appropriate order. Yes, he is aware of that. With his free hand he rakes his yellowed smoker's fingers through his hair. No, later isn't possible either. He's sick. Yes.

While he continues to sit at the garden table, his eyelids lowered, calamity begins to unfold. The word 'yes,' which ended the telephone conversation, can now take on various meanings, depending on the question that came from the other end of the line. These words could for example set in motion a huge mass of iron – a container ship due to be decommissioned that has just passed an inspection by a little-known company in one of the ports of the Far East. The matter might seem to be of marginal significance. The ship, sailing under a flag of convenience, had gone to sea with a cargo of crushed rock, according to plan but against the misgivings of its crew. The afternoon news services will bring word of a fire. At a certain moment, on every television screen the container ship will be seen in flames beneath a pall of black smoke, filmed from the air. The accident was supposedly caused by an electrical fault. The sailors – all Russian, aside from the captain – died of asphyxiation, and the shipping company was obliged to pay damages to the victims' families. Their reputation in jeopardy, the company did not even attempt to evade responsibility. It seemed that there was no way to avoid incurring losses. No one could have predicted that in F-meier's home the tension of dangerous emotions would grow, threatening destruction. Could husband and wife really have needed a spectacular accumulation of shocking events, some violent and furious disaster, to break free from the impasse in which they had been stuck, perhaps for many years? She had simply thrown him his cigarette lighter, and he had used it without hesitation at the first opportunity. Both longed for the moment when their comfortably furnished life would finally fall apart with a crash, like a sinking container ship.

Feuchtmeier. That's what this man is called. His surname, scribbled illegibly in pen on the appropriate line of the hotel form, now appears in the computerized list of guests. The narrator has checked this by calling the front desk from an ancient black windup telephone for house calls only mounted on the wall by the chest full of obsolete red fire extinguishers, umpteen floors beneath the lobby. The key that Feuchtmeier left at the front desk a moment ago is supposedly in a pigeonhole marked with a room number that could also be called, right now even, from the same antique phone, so as to hear the intermittent buzzing sound. But if Feuchtmeier has left his key at reception, he won't answer the phone.

His ex-wife is also called Feuchtmeier, like him. But he's the main user of the name printed on credit cards, engraved on the nameplate at the gate, and appearing on his ID card. Invoked on various occasions, often tossed hurriedly into the middle of a sentence, it has indicated his person in an unambiguous and incontestable way, and for this reason it would be better if, for the woman, along with the surname a first name could be found. As for him, Feuchtmeier sounds good and adequate. It probably does not come from the Fojchtmajers who were owners, let's say, of the Polish Word publishing house and printing press that was active right up until the outbreak of the second war; but it may have something in common with the easily imaginable, taciturn Captain Feuchtmeier, who wore gold-rimmed eyeglasses and who, without a doubt impeccably dressed, served for example in the navy of the Third Reich. One might mention in passing the captain's son, a difficult boy who was too much to handle for his aunts as they struggled with the privations of the postwar period. Brought up in orphanages, he did time for auto theft before he settled down. Old age found him the respectable owner of a repair shop, mending crankshafts, arguing with his wife, and watching soccer on television. He took pride in the fact that he never spared the belt, using it on his son to ensure exemplary report cards, which he keeps for old times' sake in a drawer along with his receipts.

Feuchtmeier's thirtieth birthday has long passed, while his fortieth is far enough in the future for him to believe that it will never come – after all, it was no time ago that he was playing basketball for his university team. He probably still meets with his old teammates. They shoot hoops in a local gym one evening a week, after work, and so with no detriment to their careers. Every so often one of them leaps over the heads of the others and, with a glint of madness in his eye, dunks the ball in the basket, rattling the backboard and making the steel rim quiver. Then in the changing room they crack jokes as they pull off their sweaty T-shirts. After the container ship disaster and the distress of the inquiry, which was eventually discontinued, Feuchtmeier changed jobs. In his applications he presented himself as an expert in maritime transportation. A pure formality: His name was known in the business and the circumstances of the disaster had been the subject of rumors circulating around the offices. He does what he was doing before, and again is successful, but now he works for a different company, which has expanded its share of the freightage market thanks to the damage done to its rival's reputation. Recently he has been tired. He's been sleeping poorly, and has been dreaming of a container ship split in two and going to the bottom with its cargo of crushed rocks – the image of his marriage. After the game he tends to disappear right away, going back home to the bachelor pad he found in a modernized building close to the head office of his company. One of the shortcomings of this otherwise pleasant apartment is the lack of a convenient parking garage in the neighborhood. Feuchtmeier leaves his silver five-door hatchback with sunroof, whose leather upholstery barely came clean, on the street in front of the building. He ought to reckon with the fact that one of these days it could be stolen. But he doesn't want to think about the future; he turns on all the lights in the apartment and opens a can of beer from the refrigerator. He falls asleep with it in a hot bath. When he wakes up an hour or so later, the water is cold and the can is lying at the bottom of the tub. Feuchtmeier doesn't feel like beer anymore; he'll pour himself a glass of something stronger and, teeth chattering, will go to bed. But he is no longer sleepy. Long after midnight he turns on some music – what kinds of records could Feuchtmeier listen to? – then makes himself some green tea and looks through ads for yachts in a thick advertising catalog. Outside the window the street is dark; the only light comes from signs over doorways and window displays, all without exception in the language of the narrator: Credit Bank, Dental Clinic, Irene Travel Agency. Substantial five-story buildings with rounded corners faced with granite.

As for the woman, it's clear from the beginning that the surname will create problems for the narrator. That's right, precisely that disciplined column of letters under the command of the capital F, falling into line by any predicate imposed by fate, as if it were only a matter of a drill, though they are ready for anything. But not fit for anything. For in the narrator's language it isn't possible to bring even the most adroitly mustered Feuchtmeier under the control of the feminine declension; the mechanism grinds to a halt as early as the genitive and does not work even once all the way to the prepositional and the vocative. If one were to beat a retreat and to relinquish all case-endings – Feuchtmeier's wife would herself prefer such a solution, her unfamiliarity with the narrator's language rendering her oblivious to its drawbacks – all the sentences through which her character passed would sound equally stilted. In any case she shouldn't appear under this name unaccompanied by the word 'Mrs.,' which in the narrator's language at least declines, though it's as unbending as an elderly chaperone when Feuchtmeier himself is absent – he of the expression "the Feuchtmeiers," who left and moved into a bachelor pad. In the last resort the language allows the conventional feminine form "Feucht-meierowa," ordering a subunit of the female auxiliary corps comprising two syllables to reinforce the deployed column. Only with this reinforcement will it be possible to cross the barbwire of the genitive and push on. But such a procedure, mentioned here only for the sake of thoroughness, smacks of abuse, and introduces an unwarrantable excess of familiarity, not to mention untruth. For the feminine form of the name is based on a possessive adjectival form, which expresses perfectly a narrow-minded ideal of possession and belonging, whereas it's already established that a divorce is in process. The name is a perfect fit, but assuredly for him, not for her. By itself it invariably evokes the image of Feuchtmeier, his jackets and neckties, and so out of necessity let us give the female character some kind of first name. Let's call her for example Irene, after the blue neon sign of the travel agency; why not? And so Irene Feuchtmeier. Here it might be interjected that a name carries its own weight; it encumbers like a piece of excess baggage. The wife cannot fail to notice that the husband alone has the privilege of traveling with only one item of luggage. If she wished to enjoy the same convenience, for the reasons given above she would have to be content with a first name. In fact, in a pinch the first name alone could suffice for her needs. Such an assumption inheres in the conservative nature of speech patterns, which are indulgent and humbly discreet toward Feuchtmeier, but which, in their well-worn mechanisms, aim at imposing on Irene an exemplary moderation in all things, and at overcoming the individual nature of her avid and frantic desires. Irene now lives with her father, a retired university professor, in a room in which little has changed since her school days. She graduated from ballet school but never became a professional dancer. While she had an undeniable if unexceptional talent, her endlessly practiced pirouettes would not have been rewarded with a solo career; in the best instance she could have looked forward to a regular position in the corps de ballet. Now, it is only occasionally that a dance step sets her body in motion between mirror and wardrobe. From the window of her room a small square can be seen, where women sit with infants in baby carriages – a view utterly devoid of gravity. In the evenings Irene avoids solitude. She goes out, meets with friends, usually drinks a little too much and enjoys herself, though never to the extent that anyone could hold it against her. Nor has it ever happened that a couple of friends or an old acquaintance has not driven her home. Up until now life has spared her from being accosted in the subway and from the equivocal glances of cab drivers. But the very phrase 'until now' manages, like a window left ajar, to let in among the words clinging together a gust of air that gives one gooseflesh, and one thinks with a shudder how easily the well-established state of things can change.

When Irene comes home, the boy is already asleep under a quilt patterned with small flowers in the former study, which out of necessity has been converted into a child's bedroom. She tiptoes in and stands for a moment by his cot without turning on the light. She hears his untroubled breathing. She doesn't think about the ordeals that await the boy in the future; she doesn't even want to know about the anxiety he was prey to before falling asleep. She leaves his room and goes to bed, but she does not turn out her bedside light. She doesn't feel sleepy. Sometimes she reads a book, and sometimes she just cries. Over time she even forgets exactly where the grand piano used to stand in that other living room. In a draft, that much was sure. Memory is not essential to her. Forgetting offers more freedom.

The man often remembers her still, especially at night, when he can't sleep and he stares through the window at the blue neon sign. But each of his recollections is overshadowed by an event at which he was not present and yet which nevertheless is liable to emerge fresh at any moment from his tormented memory. The shocking scene, bathed in the same blue glow as the corner of the street, is infused with the cold passion of pornographic films – it is there that he has seen the event many times; he knows how it could have come about and how it must have ended. His wife thinks that he would have been better off acting magnanimously; she can't understand why he chose vindictive obstinacy. If he had been asked about this, he probably would have said that she had no need of his magnanimity, since she had unscrupulously protected herself with deceit. Perhaps she or he still thinks that their first chance encounter will change everything. But what can they really expect? To pass one another at a crowded party, with glass in one hand and plate in the other, amid the murmur of other peoples' conversations, over which can be heard, for example, a jazz trumpet? When such a meeting finally takes place, it will not occur to either of them that something in their lives is over; rather, they will think with a dull pain that it never existed.

And that's all. It's high time for the words THE END. If the hobo with the earring is still drifting about in the background, looking for an opportunity to play his part, at this point he ought to find out that it's too late. The narrator hopes that events that have not yet happened will be called off and that he'll be permitted to forget about the characters left on the margins. After the epilogue he truly cannot imagine what more could be expected of him. He believes he deserves a respite from the affairs of Feuchtmeier, his wife Irene, and the tight-rope walker Mozhe along with his partner, whose name didn't even manage to surface before the uncomplicated plot came to an end. Because no one could be found who is not thoroughly familiar with this story, told thousands of times before. The parts, always the same ones, wait like traps into which new characters will continue to fall, irrespective of their own wishes, promises, and misgivings. The story runs things with an overwhelming force. It makes the narrator dodge about among floors and passageways until the outline of the plot is given substance. It tosses obstacles beneath his feet. In such a way the narrator comes upon a chest filled with gas masks – a new detail that appears out of nowhere and promises nothing but complications. The masks are piled high; most have no cover, and some are hanging out of the chest, hooked to the pile by their tin respirators. Further on, the hallway leads straight to some stairs, but there's no sign of an elevator, no sign of a shaft by which an elevator could descend, and no trace of a button by which it could be summoned. The absent elevator spoils the order of the entire paragraph, like the edge of a page torn out along with some of the text – the remaining fragments of sentences suddenly lose their meaning and come face to face with emptiness. In consternation, the narrator understands only that he has to withdraw and try again, but that means he does not understand anything, and it even seems to him for a moment that here there is nothing to understand. Before he collects his thoughts the automatic light switch turns off. The narrator's job is to push forward no matter what. He does so, illuminating his way with his cigarette lighter; shadows jump ahead of him into dark corners. In this manner he comes to a grille barring the way. In his bunch of keys, none fits the lock: The grille evidently does not belong to this story. Next to it, on either side, there are old hotel sofas piled on top of one another. Their pink stuffing, dirty and wadded, with crumbs of memories sticking to it, pokes out of bursting seams. The narrator averts his gaze in disgust. He looks down the inaccessible hallway and can see nothing unusual in it: On both sides of the grille, in this story and that one, there are the same low ceilings, the same shabby walls, and puddles under the moist joints between pipes. Having satisfied his curiosity, he retreats. He finds it hard now to keep his bearings and to maintain clarity in his weary mind; it is only the familiar sight of the fire extinguishers and the windup telephone that brings temporary relief. The attic filled with old copies of the Financial Times also appears in its former place, and even the window at the head of the stairs; by simply cracking open the trapdoor in the attic floor it's possible to glance at the terrace, where a restless Feuchtmeier is just on the point of putting his glasses on the edge of the table, and Mozhet is looking up at him in surprise.

The narrator leaves without waiting for the already familiar continuation. Now he is walking cautiously. Most important is that his gaze should not stray, taking with it the entire series of subsequent sentences; as long as he is passing the dark red fire extinguishers in the cold light of the neon lamps everything is just as it should be. It would seem that it's simply a matter of attention. Concentration is needed to keep a tight rein on the forces of disorder, to impose the necessary rigor, and to prevent objects from descending into the anarchy to which the unstable criteria of order incline them. But soon the narrator comes upon the chest full of limp, dirty green gas masks. He picks one up and breathes in the smell of perished rubber. A few yards further on, some steps appear; and here once again are those old hotel sofas and the grille, stubbornly blocking the way. The gas mask falls from his hands and hits the ground with a pathetic slap. Now he admits he's lost; he decides at once to call the front desk from the windup ebonite phone. He recalls the professional smile of the desk clerk and her impeccable diction. Without pleasure he also remembers the good day he was wished, and the jar filled with candies that no one takes. There's no lack of words – the narrator has at least as many of them on hand as there are candies in the glass jar; but he can find no word with which to start. And for this reason, in the end he doesn't even reach for the receiver. The condition of the plumbing and wiring indicates that the maintenance staff never visits the lower floors. Not even the maids come down; the gas masks must have been lying here for years, probably since what was once called the Cold War by the papers of the day, which are still moldering in faded and tattered piles against the walls. In the nature of things the daily routine does not reach far; there exist domains outside the responsibility of the hotel management. Nevertheless, the narrator's mind cannot come to terms with the impossibility of summoning the elevator. Yet that mind, in rebellion against the obvious, has no way out but unconditional capitulation. Having betrayed itself, it will begin to search the memory for an overlooked stretch of the way, wondering for example if the corridor with the fire extinguishers doesn't lead off from the landing, a dozen or so steps up from where the mind bears a painful scar torn out of space. The memory, prepared against better judgment to consider in all seriousness a solution such as moving the elevator half a floor up, with a suspect alacrity offers the recollection of a dozen or so steps allegedly descended; this remembrance is dim and in the light of day might well have vanished in the blink of an eye like a badly developed photograph. In the face of a glaring inconsistency bearings are lost and space disintegrates into fragments that do not match. Now the narrator must quite simply climb those steps half a floor to the elevator without which he will be unable to find his way, and which he can locate only outside his field of vision. But after the first few steps, his foot is suspended over a void and his hand freezes on the twisted handrail that suddenly turns downward, from this point accompanying other, invisible stairs that descend into a dark abyss. Water drips into it continuously; the plash can be heard. Too many steps are missing to be able to go on; all he can do is stand in place, without a single thought in his head. For in that head, too, something has caved in, leaving a gap just as vast as the one that has just appeared beneath his feet. Doubt belongs to the present tense and the present tense only; it blossoms upon it like a poisonous lily on the clouded top of a pond. At this point the narrator would do anything he can to extricate himself from the dark well of the present tense. Yet it seems that nothing whatsoever can be done; there's no sign even of a straw at which a drowning man might clutch. Perhaps the right thing to do would be to plunge into the water, take it into his lungs, and come to rest on the silty bottom – no other course can be seen. But that also is impossible. The balloon of longing keeps the mortally suffocating mind on the surface. From the very beginning, though, the narrator's position has been so unfavorable that he has nothing to long for. And thus, since he has nothing, he longs for the street cut off by a pane of glass from the hotel lobby; he longs for the country lane that can be seen over the garden fence; he longs for everything that is unattainable. The only thing that this time he has not yet tried is to look for another way out. Picking his steps unsurely, he finds his way to the attic; the old copies of the Financial Times are lying in place beneath the sloping ceiling. Here space is predictable and the ground sure. The narrator descends to the landing. Through the window of the living room he watches out of the corner of his eye as Feuchtmeier desperately tries to stop Irene. She pulls her arm free without looking at him and walks quickly away; in a moment she'll drive off in the car that is still standing in the driveway in the sun, the keys in the ignition. And she'll pick up the tightrope walker Mozhe in his striped T-shirt on which a dark red stain is spreading. The narrator's gaze does not linger on them; everything there is in any case determined in advance. He thinks about jumping out of the kitchen window on the other side of the house and walking away across the fields. The boy is not asleep at all. He knows or does not know about the scene taking place on the terrace; probably he knows, though he certainly would prefer not to. He's kneeling in the kitchen in a puddle of spilled milk. Covered with chocolate and ketchup, he's building a tower of innumerable cans of tuna, Strasbourg pâté, tomato paste, and sliced pineapple in syrup. The battery of canned goods is a symbolic image of the plague of excess that has afflicted Feuchtmeier's home. The boy is rocked by hiccups; evidently the chocolate or the ketchup has disagreed with him. Through the kitchen window a fence can be seen. On the other side of it a man in blue overalls is standing. Standing and waiting. The sunlight shining through the iron fence posts makes the same striped pattern on his clothing and on the ground. A small white cloud passing across the sky darkens the glare only for a moment. Blades of grass sway, while over them flutter colorful butterflies. The man waiting is in no hurry; it's clear that he has all eternity, and will always be able to reach into his pocket and take out his wallet, in which there is a picture of a little girl taken a long time ago, let's say somewhere in the Balkans. If he were to be permitted to say all that's on his mind, in a moment it might turn out that for example the little girl's mother – her picture is also tucked away in the wallet – remained in those parts with an infant whose picture they unfortunately did not have time to take. Where they are now is not exactly known; in any case they're in a place from which there is no way out – in some deep pit, amid a host of others lying rigid under lime and earth.

The man in the overalls has no intention of asking for pity – he will demand only what in his opinion is his proper due. It does not matter to him that his wishes cannot possibly be granted. The tower of cans comes crashing down. This is the last sound of this sequence, and it is heard on the terrace too. Now everything will start again from the beginning. And so the partner of the tightrope walker Mozhet, whose affairs are connected in an invisible yet fateful way with the scene taking place on the terrace, must once more sit in the dentist's chair, again with aching heart. Let it be the dental clinic next to the travel agency – why not? No one is presently in the waiting room, and the dentist has lots of time. He likes his patient, so he's telling her funny stories. In his opinion the damaged molar is dead and cannot hurt while it's being drilled; that is why a needle with anesthetic has not appeared in his hands. The open drawer of the filing cabinet containing patients' records reveals that Mozhe's partner's last name begins with a T. The door to the waiting room is open to let in a breeze – the day, as already established, has been hot since morning – and if the next patient were waiting, he would see the top of her head with its closely cropped red hair on the headrest of the dentist's chair. The body must bear a pain it does not understand; nothing should hurt since the tooth is dead. If it were possible to strike from the score the loud crash presaging repetition that sounds in the Feuchtmeiers' kitchen every time the tower of cans falls down, it would prevent needless suffering. And the dentist would order an X-ray instead of repeating the painful mistake over and again. But did he really not order the X-ray? It's lying on the table, in an envelope bearing the patient's name. She is called Touseulement, Yvonne Touseulement. Things could not be otherwise, since her tightrope walker is Mozhe. His name declares his freedom; it announces that maybe he will do one thing or another, but is not forced to do anything. He maybe will appear or disappear; maybe he will leave her. Her name, on the contrary, condemns her to subordination and exclusivity; whatever happens to her, nothing else is possible. Hence for him – maybe her, but for her – only him.

In the meantime the story line concerning the narrator continues to develop in a gently descending line. The narrator ought to note that the narrow wooden stairs creak underfoot, while the door swings shut of its own accord behind his back. So this is the cellar. It's spacious; high on the wall there is a vent, but it's barred. In this place Feuchtmeier keeps a set of winter tires bought cheap in an end-of-season sale, and another set that he used last winter and is still perfectly good. He keeps old, worn-out, forgotten hockey skates here, and shiny, never-used diving equipment. Is Feuchtmeier a diver? He thought once about taking it up, that's all. In the cellar Irene keeps an exercise machine – a stationary bicycle with gleaming speedometer. Once it occurred to her that it would be good to ride for fifteen minutes a day far away from the traffic. Protected by a plastic cover, her fur hangs on a coat rack; it was also bought cheap at an end-of-season sale and has never been worn. Feuchtmeier's winter jackets are hanging there too, also in plastic covers, and his overcoat, turned inside out and showing its gray-striped lining. The same one that on another occasion would go missing at the airport, along with the opalescent marble that lives in the pocket. On the shelves lie tools: an electric drill, a circular saw, hammers, chisels, files, pliers. He had need of them long ago, when he was decorating a little room with wallpaper in tiny pink rabbits. Nearby is her sewing machine and a large wicker basket full of skeins of light blue wool, supplies that she may never use up, bearing in mind that the last time she drew from them was when she was knitting baby socks. The narrator's gaze suddenly chances on a large mirror in a gilt frame that has been consigned to the cellar. It's easy to guess that it was too showy for the Feuchtmeiers' taste. It's a little dusty, but all the same everything can be seen in it, the whole interior filled with abandoned emblems of out-of-date notions and unrealized possibilities. Can anything else be seen? Has the mirror reflected the material body of the narrator? Of course, this sort of question is simply waiting its turn; several others have already been given a wide berth. The male figure captured in the oval of the mirror as if in a trap moves hurriedly aside before further questions follow about age, eye color, clothing. The narrator is hurt. He had expected his privileges to be respected, and believed that everything concerning his private life would remain confidential. Whatever he says now will sound suspicious: Could he possibly have something to hide? And so he feels deceived, exposed to prying looks. Best of all he'd like to back out of the whole undertaking posthaste. He doesn't think much of it anyway; he allows himself to be critical of its conventionality, and its artificial character irritates him. He could break free of it very easily if he were to leave this house. At a smart pace, without looking back, across the terrace even. There he might bump into Feuchtmeier, who has just caught the lighter in midair after Irene has tossed it to him. What would come of such an encounter? The smashing of the three-sided frame on which the story is pinned would cut it short. There'd be nothing more to tell. Somewhere in the neighborhood there ought to be a stop of the suburban rail line running directly to a large central station where in each corner of the main hall there stand trash cans full of half-eaten rolls and paper cups containing the remains of coffee. Amid the snarling automobiles, clanging trams and crowds hurrying along the streets it would be possible at once to start a new life as a hobo, and in this simple way hop over into a different story and live or die in it with no responsibilities. But also without privileges – as any old character. For a moment he is even sure that this is what he wants and that the one who appointed him will agree willingly to release him from all obligations. Except that the door has slammed shut and the narrator is no longer able to get out. Now he regrets his haste; he regrets the fact that he turned out to lack the perseverance to sit down on the stairs three floors above and remain there till he achieved his end and the elevator and its shaft returned to their place, even if he had to wait forever. On the floor above, the tower of cans tumbles down once again, but here the noise is muffled and hollow, like the distant echo of a storm. And in this way the narrator is detained in a dead zone of the story, amid dust-covered accessories.

In the silence that falls at this moment, there might for example ring out a short wave of simplehearted, premature applause. But it would die down at once embarrassedly, as sometimes happens during a concert when the musicians fall still for a moment to gather strength before the next movement. The piece being played by the orchestra will not come to an end until, with implacable consistency, there sound within it all the events that can possibly be contained by the form imposed upon it, no one knows by whom. And so it is not hard to comprehend why the subjects must continue to be developed, though if the question were asked differently – what are they developing for, to what end, what circumstances other than the fee paid to the musicians call into being the movement of the bows, and what patent thing necessitates the vibration of moist air in the brass loops of the trumpets – no answer could be found. It might equally well be asked why ships ply the ocean waves, why the circus audience holds its breath or bursts out laughing, why and for what is the sickly sweetness of chocolate, the banal literalness of pineapple slices in syrup, and the coarse smell of carbonated drinks. It could also be asked why Feuchtmeier lives and why Irene lives – after all, they're unable to be happy, though they need considerable amounts of water, electricity, and gasoline to satisfy all their wishes, and considerable amounts of coffee with cream, light cigarettes, and red wine. And it isn't even possible to stop at such questions. It must be asked further: Why does the acrobat Mozhe or Mozhet live, recklessly balancing on the tightrope, or his partner Touseulement, who every evening throws herself into the void without hesitation as if life held no value in her calculations, though she assigns no little importance to the durability of the fillings her dentist gives her? It should be asked why the retired university professor clings to life when he is tormented by rheumatism and has one foot in the grave; or the hobo with the earring, used to going without dinner, without a roof over his head, without a bank account. Or others – let's say it straight out – everyone, including the passers-by hurrying along. And so questions should be asked, and asked over and over. The characters fear these questions like death itself; they tremble before them, holding on if only to the handle of a china teacup, since it's easy to foresee that things are unlikely to end with questions alone.

THOUGH IT WILL NOT BE A SIMPLE TASK, let us try to imagine the continuation of this tale – for the moment, let's say, only the next paragraph, which begins with the buzzing of a fly. The buzzing ought scarcely to be audible at first; then it grows louder and louder. Only recently released from the trap that the Feuchtmeiers' hallway proved to be for it, the fly finds its way to the ceiling of their cellar and taps in vain against the firmly closed vent. Yet even if it breaks out finally into open space, it will not find freedom there, but merely another prison. And so there, too, it will agitate its wings without respite until it enters some open window. The succession of places from which there is no way out, to which open spaces also belong, is brimming with a combination of regret and desire. The world, obviously, does not end with the Feuchtmeier's cellar; beneath it there extend further floors. And if the narrator claims that he is stuck in the cellar, he is not entirely wrong, though in essence it is not there that he is stuck, but in something significantly larger that is also firmly and hopelessly enclosed. But even if he has been imprisoned in a dead zone of the story, it is only partially. For his being is given continuity by the volatile essence of longing, and not by the sluggish weight of a body that could equally well belong to someone else and be located somewhere else. The level of this essence is evened out in the long series of rooms like an arrangement of linked containers. Whereas if there should be a lack of connections, it must quite simply penetrate through the walls or ceilings. It's already drifting in places where the narrator has yet to set foot. And in this way the words 'already' and 'yet' which have no obligation to reckon with anything at all, thus demonstrate their absolute superiority over the substance of concrete and summon accomplished facts into being. And the narrator, who controls virtually nothing here, ought only to note that somewhere beneath the turf of the garden, below the layers of earth in which worms and moles dig their tunnels, lie the platforms of a local rail station. Livid graffiti appear there. Painted on dirty plaster, the initials of last names compete for one's attention: an elaborate S, which a spray paint wielding Schmidt unknown to the narrator has left stealthily on the wall, and an extravagant B put up by some Braun. They may have been the ones who tried out a new can of paint by adding a blotchy commentary to a film poster pasted up on the platform. In it the narrator recognizes the man's black sweater and the bright highlights in the woman's red hair. The film couple, John Maybe and Yvonne Touseulement, is kissing on a steeply sloping roof, beneath a firmament that has come slightly unstuck from its base.

The bench on which the narrator has taken a seat is not short; nevertheless a certain old man in a red dressing gown announces in a schoolmasterly tone that this place belongs to him alone, and has since time immemorial. He apparently deserved such a privilege out of consideration for some damp trenches where he ended up contracting rheumatism; that is, in remembrance of a past that he grumpily harps on. If the narrator continues to remain silent, in a moment they'll be joined by a hobo wearing an earring. Someone in charge of the course of events evidently casts all the parts with the same characters. Perhaps out of simple laziness, or perhaps because details make no difference to the public. Universal inattention and apathy, on which one can always count, make it easy to cover up any shortcoming. The army surplus jacket emits the odors of the dumpster, something that the narrator could not have known when he observed it through panes of glass. The hobo will demand the bottle that is supposedly hidden in a plastic bag on the narrator's lap. With an efficient wave of the hand, he's able to describe the shape of the bottle, which he has guessed at correctly; he even knows which kind it is and seems quite determined to drink the brandy even before the train arrives, in the company of the old man in the red dressing gown and possibly of the narrator himself, if the latter should only wish to join them. The hobo is prepared to assure the narrator that either way it will not be his lot to take the bottle where he is going, insofar as he is going anywhere at all. In his view, this is in any case a triviality compared to all that a person has to give up in life, not to mention life itself, for life, too, cannot be kept for oneself, for instance, by thrusting it surreptitiously into a plastic bag. The narrator sits still, his hands on the bag in question. In it is a cool bottle taken from a certain kitchen. Omniscience inspires respect. The old man praises his best student and gladly gives him credit for the course; he will not do the same for the narrator, citing considerations of an ethical nature. Specifically, it is a question here of a lack of magnanimity, a very serious failing, and so no credit will be given either now or ever, as the professor informs the narrator with a regret tinged with malicious satisfaction. The one figure that the narrator cannot recall is a grinning hipster in a studded leather jacket. He's just sitting down on the bench, pushing the other two aside unceremoniously: That's enough of that, now me. Because here everyone is simply waiting their turn, shuffling their feet; this is more or less how the leather-clad wise guy explains his loutish behavior to the narrator. As he does so he plays with a glass marble. A tiny opalescent light flashes between his fingers. But he doesn't look at the marble. His gaze taxes the narrator; it has already consigned him to the category of people who prefer to drive brand new cars of different makes moving one after another across the pages of an illustrated weekly left behind under the bench. There at least the spray can–wielding Braun and Schmidt will not intrude, and the gleaming bodywork will not be defiled by a vulgar addition. The wise guy wants to explain to the narrator the hidden mechanism of the event in which they are both taking part, revealing its course, well-established and known by heart, and its obsessive repetitions, and even telling how people keep themselves entertained here and at whose expense. Thus for instance the professor gladly has his palm greased for his worthless credits, while the hobo turns a buck from time to time with his chicanery. Though the narrator asks no questions, he might be interested in knowing what tricks the leather-clad wise guy plays on the other passengers. I slit throats, says the latter; the marble disappears, and there's a sudden click of a spring and the glint of a blade held to the narrator's neck. It'd be a pity if something bad happened; the man in the leather jacket will be content with a hundred. He's in a bit of a hurry now; his buddies have just arrived and are waiting nearby. The narrator reaches for his wallet; the plastic bag slips off his lap and there comes the sound of breaking glass. The wise guy's buddies burst out in raucous laughter, the echo of which reverberates beneath the concrete roof. The hobo waves his hand regretfully – after all, didn't he warn him ahead of time? The grinning leather-clad hipster sticks the bill in an inside pocket and walks away with an ironic bow.

And so the narrator possesses a wallet. Anticipating inquisitive questions about where he got his money, who gave it to him and what for, he ought to mention that he is incurring considerable personal expenses – the hotel, for example, is not cheap. And the one who is paying him does not expect services for free. The tips that the former hands out left and right for the tiniest thing in any case come back to him eventually. The narrator could now point to the row of ticket vending machines on the platform, from which the cash drawers are certainly removed from time to time. They end up in the same hands as the check for the commission collected by the real estate agency that took on the sale of the house with the garden; the same hands as the income of the shipping company, and the rich flow of profits from the hotel. Is it not the case that the lion's share of circulating cash ends up in the pockets of the master of all circumstances, who lies around all day in his crumpled bedding, his back turned on the world, and would he not prefer that nothing be said here about what he spends it on? And if someone simply had to know what currency these sums are calculated in, the narrator would explain calmly that it's the same currency in which he paid a hundred to the insolent wise guy. The banknote came from the envelope left for him at the front desk of the hotel. These were old Polish zlotys, withdrawn in the nineties. And let's agree right away that only old Polish zlotys are in circulation, absolutely everywhere – in the German towns where the Feuchtmeiers live, in the Balkans, even in the ports of the Far East. Various denominations, always in muted pink, pale blue, and green. The homeless denizens of the station platform do not have direct access to Polish banknotes, and so they have no need whatsoever of wallets. They may not even have any documents at all. If they bear last names, it is to their credit that they keep them to themselves so as not to worsen the confusion in the story. It's not out of the question that they, too, consider themselves narrators. The all-knowing hobo with the earring – he definitely does, and perhaps also the decrepit old professor in the dressing gown. Who would not want to be a narrator? Who wouldn't wish to have a guaranteed income, calculated in zlotys? The leather-clad wise guy, earning a little on the side with his switchblade, would not scorn it either.

At this point the narrator could give an assurance that he wouldn't have stolen a bottle from the house with the garden if he had not unwittingly gotten stuck in the ruts of other tales. It may be that all three men on the platform – each in his own way – would be glad to carry out a task that exhausts the narrator and fills him with aversion; furthermore, they do not receive one zloty for their pains. They do not have personal expenses; they don't pay for hotels or dinners; their stories are cheap. Despite this the sight of money must have nettled the two of them who got nothing. They toss scathing gibes aimed at the third, who is just disappearing with his retinue at the end of the platform: Rumor has it that somewhere or other he made a thorough mess of a job and now he's penniless and is given no more work. They recall the two unnecessary corpses from when a hotel door was destroyed; and they imagine the fury of his employer, who gave him his marching orders on the spot. In the meantime, a train is approaching the platform with a rumble; it's covered with bright zigzags of graffiti – assuredly the work of Braun and Schmidt, the elusive vandals, transparent as air. The hobo and the senile old professor enter a car along with the narrator, holding him by the elbows in case he should suddenly decide to abandon the trip. The train sets off; the response to the question of why it isn't moving in the opposite direction should be that this direction and the opposite one are of equal worth, and so it's all the same. Here then is the interior of the car; on the floor is a sticky patch gathering dirt, and there are only two people sitting on the ripped-up seats. One of them is a young woman wearing provocative makeup.

From her handbag she has taken a small mirror that reflects the highlights in her dyed red hair. Pursing her lips, she studies the outline of her flashy lipstick. Nearby sits a sullen youth with a shaved head, in a black T-shirt and camouflage pants with dangling suspenders. His grandfather stomped the rhythm of a military march in heavy boots, as an exemplary German soldier in dark green uniform. His father, for instance a locksmith, slaved his whole life from dawn till dusk. Three beers will always console: Such was his adage. He had a heavy hand. The boot and the hand will lend both men the appropriate weight. The grandfather and the father appear here as ballast; they have been brought in primarily so that the character with the dangling suspenders remains on solid ground. But aren't the face and silhouette taken directly from Feuchtmeier? The theft of a bottle of liquor is nothing compared to such an abuse. The youth does not know this. He did not pick this body for himself; it was assigned to him. He is younger than Feuchtmeier and younger than his redheaded traveling companion; he is probably called Schmidt or Braun, whatever. His wrists and forearms all the way up to the elbow are covered in deep scars; it could be wagered that many times he has grown sick of life. But not completely, since in the end he lacked sufficient desperation. It's not clear whether this couple got on the train together and if they have anything in common. It's possible that they only just met, and that they're already working out how to part on any pretext. He's toying with a dark metal object of familiar shape; the magazine keeps popping out with a snap. So there's a gun, whether the narrator likes it or not; this fact may have its consequences. The owner of the gun slowly raises his eyes. For a moment he stares at the red dressing gown, perhaps asking himself the inexorable question of why such people live and why they are tolerated. He's already stood up from his seat at the end of the car; he's approaching at an unhurried pace, swaying as the train rocks on the rails. Time to get off, bum – such words would not shock anyone now; they could be guessed at if only from the movement of his lips, when nothing can be heard over the clatter of the wheels. It's well known that red provokes. The oxidized barrel, jabbing the old man's ear, shows him which way to go. The latter would get off right away if it weren't for the fact that the train is hurtling along and the doors are locked, and so he just blinks repeatedly and tries to say something; it can be seen that he is missing several front teeth. He completely agrees with the owner of the gun; lisping slightly, he acknowledges that everywhere you go there's too much trash like himself, an old fogy in a red dressing gown. Reaching the end of the sentence, he swallows hard. The owner of the gun looks about with the glazed eyes of a madman. He moves slowly, and equally slowly considers what to do with the old man before the train arrives at the next stop. Now the hobo will interject his own comment. Ain't that a thing, he snickers, the mad have gone mad. They've joined those who'd finish off the mad right at the outset. Finish off all the maniacs, the psychopaths, the transvestites and, it goes without saying, idiots like Schmidt and Braun, too. They'd crush them beneath the soles of their hobnailed boots. The mad'd bear the brunt of it since Jews are harder to come by. And homeless winos'd be let off the hook in the end. Winos can never be eradicated. The barrel turns unhurriedly toward the hobo; the owner of the gun must want to make sure his ears are not deceiving him, especially since the clatter of the wheels muffles speech. The hobo himself didn't properly hear what he said a moment ago, so he's unable to repeat it. If that's the case, he'll have to crawl under the seat and bark when he's told to: woof woof! But the reedy falsetto he produces from his dry throat is not enough; the owner of the gun won't let up until he hears a prolonged yelping of the kind he knows well. It goes without saying that he'll get everything he demands. The ease with which a person can insist on his own way in the railroad car can only inspire disgust, and so at this moment Schmidt or Braun has had enough; he'd like to put an end to this pathetic spectacle as soon as possible. But he knows no other way than to take aim and pull the trigger. There is a deafening bang; all the witnesses of the scene close their eyes, and for a moment all they can hear is a buzzing in their ears. Then, when the moment passes and the clatter of the wheels returns, everyone realizes that the gun is just a starting pistol. Now they laugh, they laugh fit to burst, including the pretty woman in the provocative makeup, and the scruffy old man who could have died from fright and at this moment is still clutching his heart. The hobo emerges from under the seat, his clothes gray with dust, and rakes cigarette butts out of his hair. His mouth, set in a foolish grin, does not utter a single word of complaint.

In the meantime the train is moving further and further away from the point of departure, to which the narrator will have to return while he still remembers how many stops he has to go back – for the moment only one. It may be enough to cross to the opposite platform when the time comes. Unfortunately they, too, wish to get out, the hobo with the earring and the old man in the red dressing gown. The narrator walks at a brisk pace; his shoes get wet in puddles. In his haste he splashes through mud, determined to lose the other two – the tramp with the earring dogging his footsteps, and the out-of-breath professor, who every so often catches up at a trot. It may be that in his pocket the hobo carries his own bunch of keys from all the cellars he knows and all his favorite heating vents; and that he is sticking to his own route. He probably uses the gift of omniscience to find the best morsels in garbage dumps. The scruffy old man, on the other hand, undoubtedly appears as an episodic character in both stories whose plots have become entangled. Here then is a run-down neighborhood situated goodness knows how far below the level of the hotel foyer, that indifferent paradise in which the body scarcely suffers at all and has no need of sympathy, and another few floors below the beautiful gardens of summer, where structures built of expectations and imaginings come crashing down. Here is a bar on the corner, the scene of the action of unknown stories that are just as good or as bad as any others. A battered signboard bears letters in a familiar angular script. Inside there is a hum of voices; the television is on, and the local unemployed are watching a soccer game. There is a sudden hubbub in the bar: Goal! A few fans spill out onto the street; one of them gives a yodeling cry and waves a betting slip. The narrator will not hesitate for long; he'll enter the bar and mingle with the crowd. It's three to nothing. All around, people are making a racket and clinking mugs. He stands at the counter, but the other two are right by him already, and he has to order beers for them as well. He'd most like to slip away before they finish their drinks. But they guzzle their beer quickly, glancing at the TV screen out of the corner of their eye, very pleased with themselves. They may well be aware that they would have been ejected even from this bar had they not previously attached themselves to the narrator.

The only league the narrator knows is full of Polish diacritics alien to the Gothic script of the signboard. They throng the screen like the Polish zlotys in the European banks and the ports of the Far East; they flutter on the stands, appear on the illuminated scoreboard, and time and again flash between the legs of the players in motion. They run rampant, unseen, in the mass singing on the stands. Where are you off to, the two of them, the hobo and the professor in the red dressing gown, ask anxiously.

To the toilet. The bartender points the way. The narrator opens his wallet, but the hobo takes it out of his hands. He will pay when the time comes; in the meantime he orders another round. The narrator acquiesces without a murmur, remembering the payment promised by telephone for the afternoon. In the toilet there is no window. A determined search for a way out through the back rooms pays off. But the dark hallway, extremely long, takes him alarmingly far from the railroad station. Goodness knows where it leads. At its end is a locked door; none of the keys fits the rusty lock. The only way out seems to be a trapdoor in the floor. The narrator hesitantly lifts the flap and peers inside, holding up his cigarette lighter. He thinks he can make out cast-iron rungs suspended over a void. At this exact moment something soft touches his shoulder. He freezes; the lighter falls from his hand into the hole, though it isn't heard to land. It's only the hobo who was mistreated by Schmidt or Braun; he still reeks of the dumpster. Him again. No witnesses are present, and the narrator pushes him against the door; there is a crash. Most of all he'd like to grab him by the scruff of the neck and toss him like a sack of rags back down to the other end of the dark hallway; he takes hold of the army jacket and shakes the hobo fiercely, as if he wished to snap the threads of the stories that have accidentally become intertwined, but his clenched fist ends up clutching nothing but an empty sleeve. Could he have seized the other man by the throat? Yes, he is capable of that. And since he's capable of it, why should he not recover his wallet? The hobo doesn't have his wallet; in the space of a few moments he's managed to lose it, though he swears hoarsely that he's merely given it to the old man in the dressing gown for safekeeping. His eyes are popping out. Released from the iron grip, for the longest time he stands gasping. In his view the wallet would in any case be of no use to the narrator in the place he was looking at through the opening. Old Polish zlotys from before the devaluation of '95! Even jokes have their limits. He personally advises strongly against the trapdoor; it's not a good way out. What the hobo with the earring resents is not the torn-off sleeve, but the fundamental disloyalty toward others in the same boat; in a word, my friend – arrogance. He knows no greater sin than arrogance. He's really sorry about the lost lighter; he tries now to give the narrator his own, a disposable one of cheap plastic. He tries to thrust it into his hand, then into his pocket. The refusal of this gift truly saddens him, but he doesn't insist and gives up the struggle. He attempts to draw the narrator back to the bar to finish the mug of beer he left on the counter, and to face up to the events that are to come. Knowing everything but admitted nowhere, he'd be happy to enter into partnership with someone who is let in everywhere. What's that – he'll have to go back to the bar without him? He shakes his head; for certain reasons this is impossible. And in fact he does not go back. Slipping through the trapdoor, the narrator hears above his head the rasping sound of an undoubtedly rusty key in a stiff lock and the creak of a door being opened. He prefers to wait for a moment, hidden beneath the flap, in the empty space between two floors, clinging to the cast-iron rungs. It looks as though he has succeeded in getting rid of the hobo. Since things went so well, he wants to go back at once.

He lifts the flap. But now he sees rooftops, smoke coming from chimneys, walls of houses covered in black soot in the desolation of a sweltering summer. He cannot believe his eyes. Determined to return quickly through the bar to the train station, he crawls out onto the steep tin roof. He gazes around in confusion, not knowing himself what he is looking for. At the foot of the apartment building – seen from above – stands a coal cart. The Percheron that is hitched to it lifts its tail and drops brown lumps of manure onto the cobbled roadway. The day is just as hot as in the garden situated several floors higher, though the air is even more oppressive. The heated tin burns. Seeking to escape the swelter, the narrator finds himself in an attic filled with bed linen drying on clotheslines. His lighter is nowhere to be found; it's vanished. The wet white sheets seem to be steaming beneath the roof. The pillowcases exude the heady, fleeting innocence of lace. In the corner of each piece of bedding is an embroidered monogram in the form of a large F. From the attic it's possible to get out onto the staircase. From behind a half-open door on which a business card has been pinned in lieu of a nameplate, there comes the sound of a trumpet, like a golden thread uncoiling in leisurely fashion from a skein; in the space of a few bars it stretches from floor to floor. The thread must be strong, for on it hangs the fate of the unseen trumpeter, which depends on future contracts; he undoubtedly plays swing in nightclubs. The trumpeter has a short, simple name – let's say, without even looking at the business card: John Maybe. Nightclubs don't need excessive talent and are not prepared to pay for it; they're content when there is a trumpet in the band and it's played in tune; and if the owner himself sits at a table for no other purpose than to listen to the trumpet solos, he keeps this to himself. In such a way John Maybe will never get the recognition he deserves.

Lower down, the doorways to the apartments are more imposing: two on each floor, with veneered double doors, handles that inspire respect, and gleaming brass nameplates on which the names of the residents are engraved with great care, once and for all, as if the idea of moving had never occurred to anyone here. From the nameplate it can be learned who the bed linen drying in the attic belongs to. It is the Fojchtmajers'. Sooner or later this name had to reappear in some sentence; all this time it was waiting patiently for its turn. Was the Polish Word publishing house and printing press not mentioned earlier? Its additional specialty could, for example, have been theatrical posters and programs. It goes without saying that these Fojchtmajers are not and do not wish to be connected in any way with the immaculately uniformed Captain Feuchtmeier of the navy of the Third Reich, also mentioned above, commander of a gunboat sailing the southern coast of the Baltic. The captain would resent the spelling of their name. But the Fojchtmajers' name has grown accustomed to its spelling, and it should be believed that the spelling too has grown used to its sound. If the names of the captain and the publisher are juxtaposed here, the reason lies exclusively in the sequence of sentences. So the two names stand opposite one another; the initial F of the one stares at the final r of the other and vice versa, and together they impose on the story a somewhat problematic bipartite symmetry. And neither of them sounds Polish. And each is equally lengthy, and even slightly pleated, like a lowered curtain. Behind one of the curtains a gunboat of the Kriegsmarine pitches in the fog; behind the other is a throng of civilians, perhaps even Jews, half-transparent, with absent expressions. And why them in particular? This question, asked in a firm tone and requiring a response, relates to certain obligations imposed on the content by the two-part symmetry. The images should, for example, remain in equilibrium on both sides of unseen scales, thanks to their obviousness, which would be confirmed by statistics. This principle alas will not be upheld. The narrator does not consider it his responsibility. Evidently this crowd of extras was also in place and fate happened to pick them. Where did they come from? From nowhere. They are at home: They were encamped behind the curtain, in the hallways along which dismantled pieces of scenery are removed for storage after the final performance –

the sheets of plywood with the backdrops of various land-scapes and interiors in one place, the braces of untreated wood elsewhere. It's possible that from the very beginning they were somewhere between the lines. At most it might be asked why they remain stubbornly attached to their hooked noses and their sadness. This rhetorical question requires no reply, and doesn't leave the slightest space for it; but a reply forces itself uninvited into the very middle of the paragraph. It declares that they were given no choice. Existing as a semitransparent crowd and deprived of their own power to be one thing or another, in everything they have to fall in line with the words of the description. They are obliged to make do with the adjectives imposed upon them and, whether they like it or not, fill them with their own existence, as they fill the cars of freight trains that are terrifying to get into, but which it so happens they have to enter. Otherwise it will immediately transpire that their own existence is no longer possible.

Inside the apartment a telephone is ringing. It rings for a long time, insistent and plaintive. Nobody answers and it would seem that no one is home. Yes, one of the keys fits the lock. In the corner of the hall a colored rubber ball lies on the floor. The Fojchtmajers packed only the most essential things and left without warning, abandoning to their fate the sheets drying in the attic after being laundered, let's guess, by the concierge's wife. The concierge himself was drunk and didn't even see them pulling away in their black automobile. In the hallway a few suitcases were left behind, along with a hatbox and an umbrella. They were unable to pack much into their cases and had to part with their phonograph and record collection, their Encyclopedia Britannica set, their twenty-four-place china dinner service, a fur that gives off the oppressive smell of mothballs, and albums of family photographs. Even the most essential equipment that they finally managed to pack, at the last minute had to be partially abandoned for the sole reason that the luggage would not fit in the car. Setting aside one suitcase after another, those about to leave no longer remember what they packed in which case. They hope that when they come back . . . According to the principles governing the plot, they never will come back.

Upon cursory inspection, their apartment seems unexpectedly comfortable – much more so than the room with the balcony that the narrator occupied in the wing of the hotel set aside for permanent residents. The narrator notes the hardwood floors smelling discreetly of polish; the lofty, sunny interiors; and the bathroom with a window and a large china tub. He can imagine their satisfaction when they first moved into this apartment, no doubt a good few years ago – long enough for them to have grown attached to its virtues. But now, it seems, they left it at a moment's notice. The narrator lifts the telephone receiver and calls the internal number of the hotel's front desk – he's set on taking the apartment. As a consequence he wants to check out of the room with the balcony. From the receiver there comes nothing but a hollow silence suggesting in the best instance a problem on the line. It will be even better this way, without unnecessary formalities, the narrator concludes upon reflection. In the drawing room, on the turntable of the phonograph that those departing forgot to turn off, a record is still spinning with the irregular hiss of the needle. They were fond of American jazz bands. On a side table there is a circular tray; on the tray an open bottle of brandy and three emptied glasses, one with a trace of red lipstick. In a vase there is a pink rose, perhaps chosen by the person who also brought the matching box of chocolates lying next to it. So there was someone who came to bid them farewell, probably a man. Why should it not have been the owner of the trumpet living upstairs? A newspaper left behind contains reassuring news from the previous day. Clearly they gave it no credence. An inscribed cigarette lighter, a gift from the staff at Fojchtmajer's printing press on some special occasion, had been hidden under the newspaper and remained there. If Fojchtmajer doesn't buy himself some matches, he'll have to ask strangers for a light.

The narrator goes into the bedroom and opens the wardrobes; on the shelves he finds Fojchtmajer's silk shirts and underwear, all ironed and folded in neat piles. He checks the springs of the top-quality mattress on the large double bed, sits on the armchairs that stand nearby in bright covers, and feels the incomparable softness for which they were chosen. They may not have been happy, but they didn't complain; the softness of their armchairs reconciled them with their life, though not entirely and only up to a certain moment: After all, they had begun to look for a way out. In a framed photograph mounted over one of the armchairs Fojchtmajer is smoking a cigarette – the umpteenth in succession. His wife has no idea either how many he has smoked since morning – she makes no effort to count. She's staring into space from over the other armchair; she has her own frame matching the one opposite, and in it she is smiling at her own thoughts. But no one will believe that she does nothing but smile the whole time. It's possible to imagine them turning on the bedside light at three in the morning, resigned to the fact that they aren't going to get back to sleep. In recent days especially they must have been tormented by insomnia: On the nightstands on either side of the bed there are empty phials of sleeping draught. They would make some tea and sit in the armchairs, teacups in hand, discussing the worrying suspicion that they would have to relinquish their polished floors and their phonograph and record collection, and they continually cast doubt on something that was blindingly obvious given the ineluctable way in which the future tense turns into the past. They even tried to joke about this process, but their jokes were not entirely successful; they were not funny enough for them to convince themselves that they were safely beyond the reach of grammar. And so in the end, exhausted by the anticipation of leaving and by visions of an uncertain future, they changed the subject, returning to a certain betrayal, because betrayal was at least something they were capable of understanding; to certain letters that he had once read though he shouldn't have; and to lies that she could have spared him. They touched on the affairs of the Polish Word publishing house, which was stagnating below the break-even point, engaged in the hopeless resistance to particular ideas that were advancing victoriously across the entire continent; and the stock-market dealings that for many years now had absorbed all the available energy of his mind and heart, at the cost of love, naturally; and though she had to admit that up till now he had had good fortune, it had brought nothing but money. But was the income he could count on as a publisher sufficient, for example, to pay for her fur coat? Actually, never mind the fur coat – was it enough to pay the workers? In the end they fell silent, having no more to say. The man smoked a cigarette and once again considered the possibility that she may have been betraying him from the very beginning and that she had never stopped doing so; the woman was sobbing, holding a handkerchief to her eyes; and each returned separately to their solitary visions of the future. Perhaps the man was thinking that he would rather put a bullet through his brain than humiliate himself by seeking salvation at any cost. In the woman's view such a way out would be madness. And so she thought that she didn't want to know anything ahead of time. Whatever awaits her, she prefers to be taken by surprise by the course of events at the moment when there is no way out; this will spare her the need for overly difficult decisions. The Fojchtmajers had no wish to exchange well-being for hardship; she would have agreed with him that life is not worth it. What use to them is survival without comforts and entertainment? But at this point in their thinking there must have appeared a crack that was dangerous for the entire structure. Because if there are children, she thought – and he would have agreed with her – the struggle for survival is an obligation that cannot be neglected. Both of them, wife and husband, have to swallow it all, to the end, to the last drop of bitterness, without a glimmer of hope. Arrogance is not permissible here. It's quite another matter with Fojchtmajer's father-in-law, grammar-school teacher, lover of the quiet life and of good manners, veteran of the Great War, which the narrator is entitled to call the first, though in this way he also creates a second lying in wait behind the sentences. In his room, on the desk lies an obituary clipped from the newspaper: He departed just in time, readily taking advantage of the opportunity provided by a weak heart. Former grammar-school students gaze down from the walls as the narrator reads the rather wordy obituary, no doubt the work of one of them. They are lined up together, crammed forty to a frame, the first rows sitting while the back rows stand on benches. The photographs are also lined up, one year after another. All of a sudden one year tumbles to the floor with a crash. The pupils lie face down amid broken glass like fallen soldiers; on the wall nothing is left of them but a pale rectangle. A shock wave of future explosions radiates like ripples on water, reaching backwards into syntactical structures, causing them to quake. The arm of the phonograph slides off the record with a scraping sound and the turntable stops revolving. The narrator realizes that the apartment is unsuitable for him. The Fojchtmajers' children, a boy and a girl, in a costly frame under glass, do not look frightened. They still lack the experience that would help now in evaluating the situation. But pastels respond badly to shocks; the irises turn imperceptibly paler, and a tiny amount of colorful dust settles on the glass, obscuring the outlines of eyelids and cheeks. John Maybe won't wait until the walls come crashing down. He has too many crazy desires to be happy living in the ruins. Upstairs a door slams and his shoes clatter on the stairway: He's running down, taking the steps two at a time. He has an American passport in his pocket and the chance of a contract, say, in Amsterdam; he carries his tuxedo in a metalbound suitcase and his trumpet in its case; he falls asleep in trains immediately after they set off and dreams of nothing at all. He'll toss the key to the apartment through the window hatch of the concierge's lodge. There is also another key; it lies in a handbag belonging to his girlfriend, a budding chanteuse whose name – things cannot be otherwise – starts with a T.

It is by no means certain that the Fojchtmajers could have avoided the cataclysm that was hanging over their home and threatening to shatter their emotional and physical wellbeing. After all, they had played an uncompromising and dangerous game, tied as they were to the course of a story of betrayal pinned on a three-sided frame. Fojchtmajer chose not to bring matters to a head, his wife could not restrain herself, and John Maybe sailed his own course without regard for anyone else. And so it was unclear what fate these three people were actually spared or what they lost when they were forced to abandon a life that had seemed to them entirely comfortable and safe, vulnerable only to the destructive jolts of the outer world. On the dressing table, amid tins of powder and flasks of perfume, the narrator finds a photograph stuck into a thick gild-edged card folded in two. Against a background of flowerbeds in a park Fojchtmajer's wife rests her right hand on his shoulder as he stands smiling in a pale linen suit; long shadows extend at their feet. A third shadow belongs to John Maybe, who, as can be seen from the picture, is black; he stands next to them, the whites of his eyes gleaming, a shiny trumpet in his hands. On his shoulder Fojchtmajer's wife has laid her left hand. The narrator at first is a little taken aback, though he has of course heard of dark characters. The trumpet appears here as a prop in the manner of those emblems by which characters are recognized. The picture was probably taken with Fojchtmajer's camera. By whom? Naturally, by a young woman who does not appear in it. The very person the narrator had in mind when at some point he expressed the opinion that four characters is at least one too many. And indeed it is too many for a well-proportioned triangular frame neatly matching a card of hand-made paper folded in two and still smelling of fresh printer's ink from Fojchtmajer's printing press. Its trademark appears at the bottom on the reverse side. Did Fojchtmajer have to start printing invitations in order to stay in business? He did not; this was rather a favor for a friend and a small gift. So then, Yvonne Touseulement and John Maybe invite you to their wedding, to take place . . . And one need only glance at the wall calendar to see that the wedding has not yet taken place. And since this is the case, it will never come about, because John Maybe will not return. He has hopped on a train with a sudden premonition that it was his last chance to save himself before everything there goes to pieces. At the present time he's already falling asleep in his compartment. The wheels are clacking regularly, and his head is drooping and nodding in time; his body is ever further from the place he left in such haste. He is, it should be understood, safe. None of his former wives would be in any doubt of this if they were to wonder what's going on with him these days. It's easy to figure out that his former wives were black like him, gifted with slightly hoarse alto voices and an infallible sense of rhythm, though this is not enough to make relationships last. Before the date indicated on the invitation, the apartment building in which John Maybe was living will fall apart like a house of cards, leveled by the force of explosions unleashed by a Luftwaffe air raid. Every day the trumpeter will have to wake up in the early afternoon in some fictitious Amsterdam, with a dull headache, a belly full of rotting slime, and dark, stagnant blood poisoned by the relentless ease of the solutions with which life has presented him. He will swallow an aspirin, spilling cold water on his white T-shirt, and amid the chaos of radio static will listen intently to the BBC news, which however will at no point bring him consolation. For the BBC will never announce the one news item that truly concerns him. It's not important enough; it would be appropriate at most for a local evening tabloid of the kind despised by Fojchtmajer and his wife. But this news item, which would be meaningful primarily to John Maybe, doesn't appear even there, because the air raid eclipsed all other local sensations. The narrator should note, then, with the policelike scrupulousness proper to newspaper reports of accidents and scandals, that at dusk John Maybe's girlfriend found his door locked, opened it with her own key, perhaps found and read some letter that the trumpeter had left for her on a side table or the chest of drawers, certainly no more than a few lines and a signature. Then she went down to the floor below. She must have noticed earlier the absence of the golden thread spun from the trumpet and strung between the floors, in its lower registers woven into a sturdy safety net. What now will become of her, devoid of the net above which her fate was suspended? Before making any decisions, she rang the Fojchtmajers' doorbell. But no one answered. She started knocking louder and louder at their massive door with its gold nameplate, mahogany veneer, and immaculate varnish. For a moment the knocking turned into a deafening pounding. The narrator was able to observe her through the round spyhole. He could see her shining eyes and a damp lock of hair falling over her forehead. The principles of rising tension that govern scenes of this kind require that the young woman be pregnant, though the pregnancy is in its early stages and not yet visible. It goes without saying that the birth of a black child in an occupied city in which the most important document will be the German Kennkarte bearing swastikas on its stamps, is improbable in a very obvious way, and the narrator himself realizes that it should not be insisted upon. Hammering at the door ought to have tired her out. But even when she was thoroughly exhausted, the tension in the scene did not let up enough for her to return downstairs and leave on a tram. She had no choice: She went back upstairs, flung the window open, looked down into the street, and then climbed up to the attic where the sheets bearing the letter F were drying. From there she clambered through the opening of the trapdoor onto the steep roof, tearing her stockings in the process. She must have been there once before, naturally not alone. It must have been John Maybe's style to gaze at the lights of the city from high above, beneath the great firmament of the sky, just the two of them. Is that how it was on her first visit? A little giddy, they even harmonized a little, then kissed like crazy, as happens in American musicals just before the final credits. They went down to his apartment only when the evening chill made her shiver. The young woman would have preferred to stick with a nice role in a musical comedy: Drama she found offputting and a little frightening. She always thought that if life ever became truly unpleasant, she would slip away without good-byes, as though she were leaving a dull party. But after the trumpeter's departure she did not wait for an opportunity to creep discreetly out. With no regard for anything else, she jumped off the roof, her heart thumping wildly, with the key to his apartment clenched in her fist. And she fell several stories into the void, with nothing but air beneath her feet and the wind whistling in her ears. That is more or less how it must have looked, since she was found lying on the cobblestones where previously a coal cart had stood. She had died instantly, and only a tiny stream of blood ran from the corner of her mouth toward her forehead, crossing the base of her nose.

A few hours of comfort in the abandoned apartment was all the narrator could have counted on now had he been left in peace. A few hours of blessed sleep in the broad double bed before the air raid began. But now the telephone is ringing. It rings insistently and does not seem likely to give up. The narrator finds some scissors and cuts the cord. For a short time he basks in the silence, in which can be heard the soporific buzzing of flies, one, two, three of them, describing hopeless circles beneath the chandelier. But the cut cord is not enough to silence the stubborn ringing of the phone. After a moment it resumes. The narrator finally begins to realize that the call is for him. He ought to pick up if he doesn't wish to burn every bridge behind him. He who calls the shots, he who summoned the narrator and who neglected for so long to respond to letters and faxes, from time to time remembers unfinished business, from a dripping faucet to banking arrangements. At such moments he digs his cell phone out of his crumpled bedding to deal with these matters one by one.

The voice at the other end of the line informs the narrator dryly of his dissatisfaction, supposedly arising from the fact that up to this point there have been nothing but muddled descriptions of scenery, presented moreover from the wrong side: not from the front but from behind, without the slightest effort to conceal the joins between wood and pasteboard, the running paint, the drab canvas, the braces made from untreated beams that shore up the structure. Who cares if the world exists? Let it look as if it does. The deceptive impression of reality – that is what is expected of the narrator by his taskmaster. A story, like anything else, ought to flow smoothly from beginning to end, never once straying from its course. The Fojchtmajers! How did they get in here? Who gave permission to open the veneered door with their name on the plate? And to do so, what's more, using the key to the house with the garden. True, it happened to fit here, too; there's any number of doors that key will open, are there not? After all, this is a story about betrayal, and betrayal lies in human nature. The task was an easy one; there was no shortage of words, and with words anything at all can be set in motion. The narrator was to tell an uncomplicated plot culminating in the violent moment in the garden. Omitting that final scene was an unpardonable blunder, shouts the voice. But he included what happened in the garden, the narrator tries to interject; he didn't omit a thing! He suddenly realizes with astonishment that his interlocutor, so self-assured in his authority, is hopelessly misinformed. He missed the ending; a critical episode escaped his notice. And so it was his inattention that brought about the confusion. Story lines got mixed up. That's why they are now proceeding unchecked through train station and bar, headed goodness knows where. But the narrator doesn't manage to say a word; he's interrupted by the voice at the other end of the line, which knows what it knows and has its own lines to deliver. The voice asks rather arrogantly if it can count on the story being put in order, pronto. Yes or no. The narrator isn't able to answer succinctly. Stumbling over his words, he mentions the torn-up envelope he was given without a letter; the disarray in which elevators and hallways go missing without a trace; and all the instances of negligence over which he had no control. The voice calls him an utter moron, period. What negligence, whose negligence? Did the narrator expect that everything would be done for him? Has he completely lost his marbles? This question, posed in a sharp tone, could have been regarded as rhetorical, had the voice not insistently and implacably demanded an answer. The narrator will finally stammer one out in absolute humiliation, but then it will transpire that he didn't get it right, as often happens in an examination, when the candidate attempts in vain to guess what is wanted of him, and performs worse and worse. Fury seethes at the other end of the line. The narrator's interlocutor now demands explanations: Who in fact is he – a garden-variety bungler, or perhaps he's actually a saboteur, a reprobate. Yes, once again he is categorically demanding a reply. A returning wave of anger sweeps the narrator up; he starts accusing the supreme authority of sleeping through the ending, and mentions the neglectfulness and sloppiness that are the cause of the whole mess. And all this is nothing compared to the unfeeling way in which he has been cheated by being assigned a cookie-cutter story, a trite divorce tale devoid of any deeper meaning. His speech ends abruptly and is followed by an ominous silence. At last, after a long pause, the voice at the other end of the line begins to spit out words one by one: The story deserves to be told with feeling; he who pays the piper calls the tune. No one forks out for something he could do himself. There is a crash; at the other end of the line the call has been terminated. The bang of the receiver being slammed down by the narrator concludes this pathetic scene.

Yet there was something wrong with the contract from the very beginning; a hidden catch was only to have been suspected. The smell of coffee, the softness of pink stuffing, and an envelope full of money – all this in exchange for simply being present, for a scrap of testimony, almost as a gift? Since either way the narrator had no choice, they could have insisted on much more from him. And so it was not for his presence alone that he was given so many splendid promises, but for the torment of responsibility, for a burden beyond the endurance of a front man, for the inevitability of a failure in which he had gradually become embroiled. But the powers that be, it seems, have already ceased to associate any plans with his person. He still has the safety of the Fojchtmajers' apartment; he paces the hallway from wall to wall, with clenched fists, kicking the suitcases lying abandoned in the middle of the floor. Of the mirror in a gilt frame, not a word will be said. The narrator turns his gaze away from it in vexation. The rubber ball gets in his way, bumping into the abandoned luggage and bouncing against it time and again. It has to be held firmly underfoot and punctured with the scissors; the air escapes with a heavy sigh. Powerless anger, as is common knowledge, turns to doubt and despair. In the end the narrator sits on one of the suitcases. The situation offers no prospects for him other than those furnished by false contrition. In his pocket he has a notebook with telephone numbers. He's just about to reach for the receiver when his gaze falls on the severed cord. If even this doesn't prevent him from making a connection, the deciding factor will be a busy signal: He who allotted him his task is not waiting for his call but is already talking with someone else about something else. It gradually becomes evident that the narrator's position has undergone a change. It has worsened, considerably so, though only a few paragraphs earlier he believed it could get no worse.

Overcome by concern for his own skin, he even considers running away, at first not entirely seriously; to test the waters, he imagines searching for another hiding place after leaving the comfortable apartment, the address of which must surely be known to those up there, just as they have the phone number. And what if it isn't a story about betrayal? A frightening thought. From one moment to the next, escape increasingly seems to him the only sensible solution. Without his documents, left in the hotel room with the balcony, without money, without plans for the future, without much in the way of hope, he tries one more time to retreat across the attic filled with white bed sheets hung out to dry and through the dark back rooms of the bar, the same route by which he came here from the train station. But the trapdoor leads invariably to the roof. Below, the doctor from the ambulance is pushing his way through a crowd of onlookers to write the death certificate; here and there can be seen the dark blue uniforms of the pre-war Polish police. The narrator gingerly makes his way to the opposite side of the roof. Looking down over the eaves, he notices a car, a silver hatchback, which at this very moment is pulling up with a screech of brakes in front of the apartment building. It must be said that they didn't make him wait long. The car mounts the sidewalk with one wheel; out of it jump two men in gray-green uniform jackets thrown straight over blue denim overalls. With a disconcerting emblem on their caps, and with cocked guns, they hesitate in front of the entrance. It's clear that this is the first time they have appeared in these military outfits, and they've not had time to figure out how they should behave. The sergeant accompanying them is the last to get out of the car. For a moment he juggles an opalescent marble in his hand as if he were still making up his mind about something; then he steps forward. In the premature colors of the Wehrmacht they run up the unseen stairs. Evidently there were not enough dark blue uniforms to go round, as they were needed at the same time to complete the picture of confusion on the other side. For a long time they search the unlocked, deserted apartment; in the end they burst into the attic, amid the bed sheets blocking their view. They drag them off the clotheslines and trample them underfoot in their hobnailed boots. They poke into every corner. In the meantime a police captain is calmly studying the windowsills in the trumpeter's apartment with a magnifying glass, looking in vain for a trace of a woman's heel. He has gone through the handbag she left behind and has found her purse, compact, notebook, and a card from the dentist's. The dentist has been located immediately and brought to the scene of the accident to confirm the identity of the victim. Concealed on the roof, the narrator cannot see what is happening on both sides at the same time; this is prevented by the ridge of the roof, which divides the space in two. And so on one side there is a five-door silver-gray hatchback with sunroof, on the other the dark blue police. Sounds come from both places at once, but do not intermingle. On one side is a diffuse hum of voices, on the other the shouts of the soldiers, the clatter of boots and the sudden report of a gun. But there is no tunnel by which the sound of the shot could reach the other side of the story and be heard by the plainclothes police captain and the dark blue policemen bustling about there. One of the privates in gray-green opens the trapdoor and looks around on the roof. It's not clear whether he has missed what he was sent for, or whether for some reason he would rather pretend not to have seen anything. A long time passes before they reappear on the street, dragging the gramophone to the car. The sergeant gives them an earful and urges them to get a move on. They go back inside, bring out the suitcases that had been abandoned in the hallway, and return once more for the portrait of the children, perhaps because of its valuable frame. The sergeant carries it out carefully, since pastels don't respond well to shocks; while the two privates follow behind with armfuls of Fojchtmajer's silk underwear and shirts. Now they're getting into the car. They turn on the engine but don't set off at once; first they help themselves to some chocolates from the pink chocolate box. They can be seen through the open roof of the car, passing the box around. Where will they go? Before the car disappears around the corner of the street, the sergeant in the army cap will turn back and without taking aim – nonchalance is permitted, since here nothing depends on meticulousness – will fire his pistol in the direction of the chimney from behind which the narrator is peering out. A dry crack is heard; the narrator's body suddenly jerks as if struck by a whip. The bottle of brandy he has taken falls from under his arm. It rolls down the tin roof and shatters loudly on the cobblestones somewhere below.

This could not have been foreseen. There wasn't meant to be a gunshot wound in the story the narrator was telling, especially one that he himself would sustain. But he has in fact been wounded. He acknowledges this reluctantly, because the fact of the injury points unambiguously to a body; it proves that the narrator possesses one. He has a beating heart, sensitive kidneys and liver, soft skin, delicate muscles and dark red blood – everything that, not without a certain disquiet, can be studied on the pages of anatomical atlases. The suggestion that things are otherwise, present in the background from the very first paragraphs and fed by what was left unsaid, all at once loses its convenient, noncommittal quality and acquires the ordinariness of that which is spoken outright, the inertia of concrete statements, heavy as bricks. Suddenly filled with substance, the illusion loses balance and falls over. In this way the discreet insinuations of the narrator turn into brazen lies. This unexpected turn of events, shedding light on a troublesome issue, lends his earlier intimations the quality of playacting and exposes them to ridicule.

The narrator bears a body – like every one of the characters, like the hurrying passers-by carrying their burden along the sidewalks. He hid this fact doggedly, not shrinking from bare-faced prevarication. Now he would like to say something in his own defense but cannot, somewhat dazed as he is, and lying spread-eagled on the steep roof. The body, barely grazed, is bleeding unrestrainedly. The body has its own weight and is afraid that if it grows weaker, it will follow the bottle and slip off the roof. It's drenched in cold sweat; the pain does not give it a moment's respite. It sees no escape, no future beyond bleeding, no hope of anything better than a slow demise. The body realizes in despair that it was permitted to relish the smell of coffee, to experience the softness of sofas and the caress of soap and warm water, only up to the point at which the world pulled the ground from under its feet and the air from its lungs. Vulnerable and cowardly, always with something to lose and always prepared to yield to pressure, sell itself, abase itself, to pay any price to be saved, it was unable to prevent a thing. While it still stood on its feet, it tried to negotiate favorable con-ditions for itself. Yet the time will come when this aching body will have nothing more to offer, and its concessions will prove worthless. And it will have to give everything back; it will be left only with whatever space in the world it manages to gather beneath itself as it lies insensate.

But when the moment passes and it becomes clear that it was not yet its last, the heart gradually calms down and the body already starts to look for something better. If the narrator were to drag himself downstairs, he could probably have his wound dressed by the doctor from the ambulance; but the dark blue police would not spare him their official questions and sensational hypotheses, not to mention their habit of checking documents. He squeezes through the opening of the trapdoor; with his good hand he pulls a monogrammed sheet from one of the clotheslines and, with the aid of his teeth, he fashions a makeshift bandage. The loose sleeve of his jacket dangles at his side; beneath its open tail his arm hangs inertly. Somewhere round the corner there must be a doctor's office. The narrator decides to look for it, disregarding the fact that he has no wallet. In any case, the banknotes it contained would have been useless here. On the far side of the attic there is a wide-open door with its lock shot off, a memento of the recent presence of the three figures wearing German uniforms. He reaches the door, staggering and bumping into the beams of the sloping ceiling. Beyond the door another attic can be seen. From there one can access the staircase of the neighboring apartment building, which is decorated in marble, with an elevator lined with mirrors. The narrator touches the buttons of the elevator, doubting whether any of them are meant for him. Certainly there exist first-aid stations for the wounded, for those shot by the soldiers in the gray-green uniforms of the Wehrmacht. Frenetic surgeries where no one asks any questions. But the nearest such place is undoubtedly situated many floors beneath the foundations of the apartment building; for the heavier the burden of life, the lower it descends. The narrator, who has grown familiar with the way of things, can imagine the confusion, the stale air, and the uproar that reign there. He selects a button marked First Floor. The mirrors surround him on all sides; this time he has nowhere to retreat in protest at their idle inquisitiveness. Here he will no longer be able to evade the awkward question of his reflection. Everything can be seen in the mirrors: the parting on the top of his head; the white collar, no longer fresh; the knot of the necktie. The tie is crooked, and the narrator straightens it with his good hand. Above the tie, gold-rimmed glasses. The discolored fingers of a smoker rake through his hair. That's right. There's no sense denying it: The features, silhouette, and gestures are easily recognizable. In general, the narrator is embittered by the lack of privileges that he ought to enjoy; he is touched to the quick by the supercilious way in which his privacy has been invaded. He would prefer to remain silent, but since certain inconvenient details have come to light, he is forced to admit that the body does not belong to him alone. It was issued to him, like a hospital gown or an army greatcoat. He can only speculate as to where this appearance came from, and guess whose image was the basis for all the copies in circulation.

He cannot refrain from asking bitterly who is actually in charge in this space, who has placed the various figures in it, who set the events in motion. It may be that the principal matters are resolved in the mechanisms of grammar, in the inscrutable moving parts of the elevators. He who slept through the scene in the garden, the lavishly illuminated climax, is probably still under the illusion that nothing can happen here without his knowledge and without his will. Occupied with his own affairs, he only infrequently and sparingly gives his distracted attention to the story, and his overweening pride leads him to believe that this is sufficient, and that anything he touches, however casually, will immediately become transformed into precious metal. And yet he does not know everything that goes on behind his back, between the lines of the text, in the dark corners behind the paragraphs. Story lines that he ordered to be concluded and cut off are unfolding on the quiet – proof that his will does not determine everything. Where now is the black automobile loaded with luggage? Perhaps in a ditch, out of gas, pushed aside by the throng like all the other cars. Fojchtmajer and his family are among those wandering the roads on foot, sleeping in barns; the autumn is a warm one. Until winter comes they can manage like this. In any case, a simple accident will free Fojchtmajer from the arduous obligation of surviving the winter, and the frost will never touch him. Before it can strike, soldiers in gray-green uniforms will appear on motorcycles – two privates and a sergeant. The cause of the far-reaching disruption that arises suddenly from their presence may turn out to be some denunciation linking the person of Fojchtmajer with the Polish Word publishing house. For someone up above, this could serve as a convenient excuse to close this bothersome story line once and for all. At the decisive moment

Fojchtmajer's wife disowned him without hesitation, and so convincingly that she rescued the children from danger. He was present at the time, and appreciated the ease with which she lied; he felt relieved and grateful. And so his wife and children are in the crowd, while Fojchtmajer stands to one side now, his hands raised, under guard. Betrayed, three times betrayed. He will exchange a word with one of the privates; his wife waits anxiously for a sign, for after all she loves him as much as she is able. With a helpless smile Fojchtmajer shakes his head: Nothing can be done.

The elevator, as could have been predicted with even the faintest idea of the way of things, will not stop at the first floor. It will transpire that the first floor was never in the running as a scene of the action; the elevator descends lower and lower, moving ever more rapidly, till it comes to a stop with a sudden jolt. It is only now that the door will open. It isn't the only elevator in the large lobby where the narrator has found himself. Steel doors slide open and shut; now here, now there, small red lights flash over them. The tiled floor is strewn with handfuls of loose straw; sheaves of straw lie about, and straw mattresses block hallways that lead in every direction, echoing with moans and permeated with the smell of disinfectant. Let's say that the exhausted doctor, the only one in the entire field hospital, in civilian life was the youngest assistant of the senior registrar in a university hospital; he had hoped to specialize in, for instance, gynecology. Instead of this he is battling gangrene with the aid of a surgical saw, assisted by a perpetually sleep-deprived orderly whose suspenders dangle beneath an ill-fitting white coat. The orderly is more vigorous all the same; he handles all the paperwork himself. What can they talk about, looking hard at one another through reddened eyes? Between them lies a stack of forms completed in the careful handwriting of a postal clerk only recently forced to give up his first ever appointment. The doctor's gold-rimmed glasses flash. He is indignant. This patient isn't dead yet, he remarks, thumbing through the forms; nor this other one, nor that one. Later there'll be no time for paperwork; in this matter the orderly is undeniably right. With a vulgar curse, the doctor signs death certificates in advance. Formalities are easy. Nothing matters to those lying on the mattresses, gasping for breath; they no longer have any other desires. Their massed breathing is interspersed with whistles and hisses, then turns into groans, the bubbling of loose coughs, sobs, and hoarse rattles, interrupted all of a sudden by snorts that sound like giggles. The less seriously wounded slurp soup from tin bowls. On these lower floors of the hotel the body seizes the moment, greedy and certain of nothing. Personnel and freight elevators go up and down, bringing ever more con-signments of wounded. Buckets are filled with bloody dress-ings fashioned from bed linen, some with shreds of lace still attached to them – improvised bandages that in most cases were of little avail. Over the refuse there is a buzzing – flies have gathered here from all the floors. Those that were looking for an open window and those that kept circling beneath lamps. They are always drawn to places where life is harder. At the end of their journey hangs flypaper. They squirm about on it in vain. They do not realize that the long series of rooms from which there was no good way out ends precisely here.

Stretchers glide by bearing discolored fatigues, school uniforms, pure wool suits riddled with bullet holes, flowery cretonne frocks. With an infallible eye the orderly tells life from death and points the bodies in the appropriate direction. One of the stretcher bearers limps as if he were dancing. He miraculously managed to save his walkman and headphones and he himself also miraculously survived, plucked out of some African backwater from which no one else emerged alive. The other stretcher bearer steps behind the first, seeing nothing, clinging to the stretcher. From the plight he found himself in, probably somewhere in the Caucasus, he saved everything except his sight, and now he raises his feet high, afraid of stumbling. They go back and forth; at a certain moment they will bring in Fojchtmajer's wife with a round hole in the back of her head, dragged by a military policeman from a cart full of people and shot to death on the spot. The children are riding on among strangers. The narrator will find it hardest to conclude the matter of the children. Since the Fojchtmajers stopped at nothing, accepting every kind of humiliation, willing to bear anything for their sake, the children ought to be spared. But the lowest floors of the hotel know no pity. Here no one has the time or the inclination to worry about individual fates. There is no way of counting how many women have passed through the place, each with a round hole in the back of her head, taken from buses and trains in which their children continued on. In the lobby there is a feverish commotion: The center of the room must be cleared, right away. The walking wounded hurriedly push the last mattresses against the wall, for those lying on them are delirious from fever and cannot help. Gazes stray upward and are lost beneath a ceiling so high it cannot be seen. But they at least latch onto a dark shape gradually descending ever lower. A substantial hull can already be made out. The orderly makes a call, trying to arrange something; he shouts into the receiver, but at the other end of the line it seems he cannot be heard. A German gunboat slowly drops onto the floor, a rusty white waterline on its side; it is full of dead sailors in navy blue uniforms and round caps bearing the inscription Kriegsmarine. The boat settles with a groan and tilts over, creaking at its seams. The captain, immaculately dressed, is still on the bridge; his wide-open eyes no longer see anything through his gold-rimmed glasses.

Here the story branches off in every direction; the hallways leading from the lobby seem to have no end and one can imagine innumerable further branches, just as overcrowded and stinking just the same of disinfectant; they gradually enter the territories occupied by the mortuary and governed by its laws. The transitional zone includes the resting place, for instance, of unshaven Russian prisoners of war staring with glazed eyes into the void. Accustomed since childhood to sleeping in gray underwear, to wretched canteens, and to rules and regulations that outlaw expressions of freedom, they shouldn't complain about their captivity, even if they have died from hunger and cold. No more mass parades await them and they lack for nothing. Their rest is shared by German prisoners of war, who were fortunate enough to survive the confusion of battle and then froze in the ice and snow of Kamchatka. They set off for the east when the grass was probably still green. It was only in the newsreels that it turned out to be gray. Clouds swirling like high seas chase across the sky. Somewhere outside the frame is concealed a symphony orchestra; the bombastic rumble of timpani and the crash of cymbals sound the loudest. The stiffened bodies no longer hear anything now. They melt slowly; at times a transparent tear flows from beneath an eyelid and down a cheek. The story has no sharp boundaries. That is why it must include so many dead. Neither the prisoners of war nor the civilians have been granted the reprieve of an easy death. Their spilled blood soaks into the earth, and with it despair. Wounded feelings do not decompose quickly; their traces contaminate the soil for years afterward, like a fatal deposit of lead. Mention should be made of all the stories of walls and ceilings, weighing down like an inconsolable sense of wrong. Of the torment of unutterable boredom from which there is no longer any escape. Chance passers-by, torn by the flashes of explosions from crowds pressing along shopping streets, lie in black plastic bags stacked in layers. The dead, caught in the trap of the same story as always, in the end are left with nothing but their bodies, dispossessed of all rights. All are made of the same clay, with the same parting on the top of their heads and fingers yellowed from smoking. They are distinguished by their memories, but the memories are inaccessible. The body is like a millstone with which dreams are weighed down so they will drown once and for all. Unimaginably lonely narrators would never be permitted to have a say in anything except grammatical forms; it was their lot to bear responsibility without a trace of influence on the course of events, and now they are filling cellars the length and breadth of the world, all the way to the seas: the Blue, the Green, the Yellow, and even the White – all resembling the Dead. The waters do not mix. The bodies rest on the bottom, tangled in seaweed.

The narrator sees that the story has slipped out of his hands, or so it seems to him. From the beginning it pulled in its own direction; everything in it was determined ahead of time. He has run out of strength and hope; he has a desire to fall asleep with his head resting against the wall, nothing more. Instead of which he will become a messenger. He thrusts into his pocket a plan penciled on the back of an unused form. Apparently up there, on the next floor, it's possible to get a better night's sleep in a vacant camp bed with real sheets. In the meantime the orderly is sounding the floor and gazing at the doctor. Neither of them expects the floor beams to hold out much longer. A team of welders must be found immediately to cut open the hull of the sunken gunboat. Underneath there is nothing else, no foundations, only a bottomless chasm; and if the thin floor gives away, battered mattresses and hospital screens will go flying in disarray into the chasm of these lower heavens, and with them surgical instruments, used bandages, and slop buckets splashing their contents about in the mad rush. The map consists of a sketched fragment of the labyrinth of hallways, with an arrow indicating the place where the addressee of the message, dressed in blue overalls, should be sought. A second arrow shows the location of the promised camp bed. The outer door of the freight elevator closes behind the narrator. In the wan light of a dusty bulb any button can be selected – naturally it has no significance whatever. The narrator recognizes the cracked pane of the inner door. Now the elevator moves upwards, and along with it the sentence in which it appeared for the first time, and the last one in which it was rediscovered by chance.

To the question of why it does not stop at the next floor, where the narrator might run across the welders capable of averting a disaster, the answer should be that all floors are of equal worth. It is known that from the very beginning the elevator did not stop at every one. Nobody here could see beyond what is visible; the narrator is subject to the same limitation. It doesn't seem as if the stops of the freight elevator are governed by someone's will. They are decided rather by the tangle of wires tumbling out of an instrument panel, arbitrary electrical impulses that follow various paths in their own particular order. In this way the Warsaw Uprising does not break out and is not suppressed, and there do not appear drunken officers of the Soviet secret police hammering their fists on the table. There are no cheering crowds with red banners, nor mass songs, nor tanks driving out onto sleeping streets in a snowbound winter. Selecting a floor, the elevator regulates the movement of adverbial phrases, while they in turn trim the story lines short; restricting time and place, they dwell on manner and pass over cause in silence. They reduce the plot to a minimum. But it is not they who are the essence of the invisible structure, just as it is not the ropes strung over the abyss, nor the ocean currents, nor the precipitous lines of the graphs of market reports in the Financial Times. Its core and foundation may turn out to be the predicates of sentences, which as a rule are unfeeling and, like judicial sentences, irreversible. No one knows where they come from; the narrator does not know either. They become visible only when they are firmly fixed in tenses; they take the space of the sentences into their possession. And when they pass on, a void is left behind.

The elevator stops with an unimaginable clatter at the train station. At the end of the platform, far in the distance, there can even be seen the colorful splash of a poster with a couple kissing on a steep rooftop; the image can barely be made out in the foreshortened perspective. The rails rumble; it is the train, traveling in a circle so that the madman with the starting pistol can continue to bully the old man in the red dressing gown and humiliate the hobo, all in the presence of the girl with the provocative makeup. Beyond the door of the elevator there open up expanses of possibilities that will never be fully explored. But the narrator is not curious about them. He guesses that he ought not to leave the elevator as it stops at successive floors. At most, at the next one he'll block the door with his foot, lean out and, holding up a cigarette lighter – a commemorative gift, though not for him, and never mind who it was from – he will see a perished gas mask abandoned by the door. Things will return to their places: the shoddily plastered walls, the low ceilings, the dust-covered floors with puddles here and there over which droplets of rusty water hang from joints in the piping – if one falls, another will immediately take its place. Straining one's ears, one might hear the tower of cans crashing down in the house with the garden. Many floors above, the dingy landing remains in place, seemingly inaccessible; yet the elevator in fact stops there too, opposite the familiar door marked with a half-effaced figure of a man, as if in a dream. The external world puts up no more resistance. If the unexpectedly happy ending does not arouse the narrator's suspicions it is only because he is collapsing from exhaustion. But he is already on the landing; he discards the map scribbled on the back of the form, and the elevator takes it away, back into the depths of the dark shaft. The narrator isn't even sure if at this exact moment the lower floors still exist. On the upper floors this can never be known for certain. And if the lower floors have already caved in, that means the remaining floors are now the last, in the grip of fever and commotion. But in a place where leather sofas exude the cool tranquility of affluence, it can be believed to the very end that the upper floors will never become the lower ones. The narrator, too, wishes to believe this. He looks for his keys. Where have they gone? Were they left down below, along with his jacket? He has them. They're not lost – he's found them in the pocket of his pants. He doesn't know if he should first open the room with the balcony or the door to the bathroom. He opens the room. He immediately becomes aware of a sizeable dark object on the bed. A little evening light falls on the object from the balcony window; it looks like an instrument case. The figure seated in the armchair the narrator notices only after a moment. So someone must have been waiting for him to come back, for goodness knows how many hours, till finally he fell asleep. His hunched back can be seen. A hand hanging over the arm of the chair is almost touching the floor. The hand is black.

It's John Maybe, a hardened alcoholic. He has not known happiness in life, that much is evident. He's burdened by his wasted talent, by the torments of loneliness, and by the indisposition he has suffered in the mornings for many years, and which aspirin no longer alleviates. He is wearing an overcoat bought from a thief at a flea market; the sleeves are too short. The narrator recognizes the coat. He even knows that the lining has gray stripes and that the marble is no longer in the pocket. John Maybe would no doubt like the narrator to change something in his past; he believes that the story has not treated him fairly and that he deserves at least one more chance. He believes that a minor revision will not cause any trouble. All that needs to be done is to cancel the departure of a certain train, for example on the pretext of the strained political situation. Every word of his is predictable, even the rancorous tone that accompanies the presumed beginning of his speech; at its end, which there is no need to cite, it would turn to bitter sarcasm. The narrator withdraws quietly so as not to wake the intruder. He should now inform the front desk that some stranger has broken into his room from the balcony, and no more. He could go down there right away – he'll just quickly unlock with a grating sound the door marked with the faded figure of a man. The bathroom, undoubtedly as dilapidated as the landing, would spare no one the sight of its antiquated white tiles and cracked urinal, but the light bulb has burned out. Sure, the narrator uses the urinal; did he even deny it? He couldn't have. He's entered many bathrooms since he left his room in the permanent residents' wing this morning: the one on the first floor of the house with the garden and the one in the back room of the bar. He was in a handsome bathroom with a window and a china tub. And even in the hell of the field hospital located on the lowest floor of the hotel he went behind a screen where there was a stinking bucket. Would it not be easier to live without a constantly refilling bladder, without that painful discomfort, ridiculous in its repetitiveness, and familiar to the point of tedium to all the characters? The urinal, then. The narrator finds his way in the dark without difficulty, but his fly gets stuck. His wounded arm is of no use now. But the other has managed somehow to unfasten the button, and all would be well were it not for the darkness, were it not for the vague anxiety that exudes from it, intensifying from one moment to the next. The narrator knows the rules and at this point could already predict that he will never return to the room with the balcony. He ought to come to terms with the loss of his comfortable bed, together with his pajamas, which – this much is certain – will fall into the hands of the black trumpeter. With one hand it's harder to fasten one's pants than to unfasten them. The narrator struggles for a long time with the loop of the button. Hurry up, we're on in a minute, someone whispers in his ear, planting an oversized bowler hat on his head.

The narrator's heart sinks. Whose arm is leading him? All around there is a blinding glare, but the bowler hat has slipped down over his eyes. Nothing can be seen. Yet drumrolls are heard. The band plays a flourish. The other sound, resembling the roar of foaming waves, is applause. A moist whisper at his ear informs him that the tightrope walkers' act has just finished. Mozhet has recently been working with Irene. Yvonne was better, but what of it, since she's dead. So which of them was eating breakfast with him in the hotel? Bright, cheerful

makeup hurriedly paints a broad crimson smile on the narrator's cheeks. In his memory the name of Irene Feuchtmeier is
lit up, originating from a blue neon sign; the narrator should
admit that the news has taken him by surprise. But he cannot
linger over it even for a moment. Propelled toward the lights,
he'd like at the very least to have his fly fastened. But this can't
be done. He trips over something soft. It's his guide's leg, held
out deliberately. The narrator flips over and lands on his nose in
the yellow sawdust, losing his glasses. A burst of laughter rings
out. The echo gives an indication of the size of the place; it's
rather large. The guide's helpful hand sticks the bowler hat back
on his head as he struggles to his knees, brushing sawdust from
under his collar. He gropes his way to his feet, his crimson grin
stretching from ear to ear; then he falls down once again. This
time the guide has stepped on his pants leg and given him a
clownish boot up the backside. The narrator has no choice but
to get up again, this time without his pants. Despite the shame
it's easier this way; the hand that had to hold the pants up is
now freed and has already managed to straighten the battered
bowler hat in a gesture closely resembling an obsequious bow.
Bewildered, he stands in his checkered boxer shorts amid the
whistles and the applause. The perimeter of the ring extends
around him. Beyond it are rows of seats, and in the seats the
audience, all lined up. Nearby the wise guy in the studded
leather jacket is prowling around – the one who apparently
once botched a job and was given his marching orders – a man

of all work whose powers are not entirely clear. It seems he has finally been forgiven the two unnecessary corpses; it was evidently hard to get by without his brisk resourcefulness, devoid of any scruples. He was the one who put the bowler hat over the narrator's eyes in the bathroom. Now, making faces for the audience, he makes a show of bringing in a chair. Sure enough, the narrator is to climb onto the chair to retrieve his glasses, which are hanging from a wire, their gold rims glinting. When he is up there he will suddenly remember something. A monologue? Who would have need of a monologue? Entirely sufficient are the shrill exclamations with which the wise guy gladly takes over his part – signs of comic terror that the narrator refuses the audience when the chair is pulled out from under him. The wise guy applauds him enthusiastically: bravo, bravo! He's obviously enjoying the game; he can't stop, and is already dragging in a rickety stepladder. To the delight of the audience the narrator now falls from the stepladder, waving his arms in every direction. Battered and bruised, but still wearing his garish crimson smile, he places the recovered glasses on his nose. Now he can see clearly. In the front row sits the retired professor with the small boy; next to him is Feuchtmeier, yawning and surreptitiously reading a newspaper, undoubtedly the Financial Times. The boy can't sit still; he's fidgeting restlessly, picking wads of fluffy pink stuffing from his quilted vest. He's probably a handful in preschool, too. Gusts of wind whisk away the pink stuffing and lift it overhead in streaks of light toward the realms of shadow. There it disappears without a trace, in the blink of an eye transformed into a dark fleecy dust. There's nothing more full of promise than fragrant pink stuffing, and nothing more hopeless than a ball of dust trodden underfoot.

Somewhere in the audience the hotel receptionist is glimpsed in the company of a soldier of the Wehrmacht and a dark blue Polish policeman. She's sitting between them, on the best of terms with both. Her shift at the hotel is evidently over. Amid the young women with short-cropped hair dyed red is the sullen youth with dangling suspenders. Elsewhere there is the all-knowing hobo with his torn sleeve and his earring, a sign of illusory freedom. There's also the old man in the red dressing gown. And the auto mechanic, head of the household, who boasted his whole life of having a heavy hand. They're almost all there, even the two arrivals from the Balkans, a pair of workmen in blue overalls, probably brothers. With them is the girl from the photograph. Clearly their complaint eventually reached where it needed to; perhaps it was decided that two men who have nowhere to go back to may always come in useful. Here and there is a solitary black man, dark as the night, though these, too, are only appearances, a sort of costume. Among the dockers from the ports of the Far East are groups of Russian sailors of the merchant navy who after the show will immediately set off once again in search of ever more outlandish adventures. Kind-hearted black women exchange comments and slap one another on their fat thighs, continually laughing in raucous and slightly hoarse voices. People never want to be reminded of their own suffering. All they want is to be entertained. The wise guy will not let the narrator rest; he already has him by the collar. From beneath the bowler hat he pulls out a large polka-dot handkerchief. He tweaks the narrator's nose painfully; the French horn sounds out like a ship's foghorn. The narrator of course tries to break loose; he swings his legs in place to the rhythm of a ragtime played so unevenly it sounds as if the band has begun a crazy chase among the instruments. All of this pleases the children mightily. They even ask for the hilarious scene with the polka-dot handkerchief to be repeated. But the end of the act is drawing close. A well-aimed slimy apple core hits the narrator in the face. The wise guy in the leather jacket twists his neck with an iron grip, and forces him to bow over and over. The audience warms up again, because in a moment the elephant is to emerge from the wings. From the better seats its trunk can already be seen. Drumrolls sound. The audience goes wild. It's obvious that everyone was waiting only for the performing elephant.

The band plays and the elephant, raised on its hind legs, dances a tango; its trunk sways to the rhythm of the music, and a splendid pink bow flutters on its flat forehead. The leather-clad wise guy cracks a whip for effect. The audience grows quiet, mightily amused that the elephant is dancing solo, and that it keeps misstepping. Festoons of colored lights are turned on around the ring. The standing ovation goes on and on. From one bar to the next the tango turns into a circus march – it isn't clear exactly when, as hardly anything can be heard. The chaotic finale is drowned out in a storm of applause and cheers. The elephant makes a triumphal lap of the ring. In a moment it will be led offstage. The leather-clad wise guy suddenly leans out from behind its immense body, makes a face and in lieu of a farewell throws something at the narrator. A crumpled ball of paper. The narrator smoothes out the letter, once torn up and now taped back together. He would read it, but it's too late. As the spotlights go out, everything is swallowed in darkness.

The sentences will be shorter and shorter. They do not have the strength anymore to break away toward the expanses of the future tense. They contain less and less sky and more and more fog and earth. Hardly anything is possible any longer. And no truth will appear until the secure forms of the past tense impose order. Toward the end, the story descends into chaos; words go missing, lost between the lines. The life slowly ebbs out of them. The narrator had not thought about this before. Made weary by the burden of the story, he had not asked himself what kind of future awaits him when all the story lines come to an end. When the circle is complete. When the last of the sentences falls silent. And the last bar of the circus march. The band plays ever faster, as if it were being pursued. Let those crotchets be allowed to sound out, for goodness' sake! But the musicians are already leaving; the final chord has vanished somewhere, unheard by anyone. They carry out their instruments: French horn, bugles, and side drums. But where are the violins? Those that at the beginning sent the sound of open strings into space? It was they who imitated the buzzing of flies, starting with the first one hatched from some word to show the way. Could the violins have slipped away without waiting for the finale? The memory does not stretch far back; in it sounds have already been erased. Nothing more will be seen or heard. The silence is like a boundless ocean in which worlds are submerged. Against darkness and inertia no one has ever yet prevailed.

Moving Parts by Magdalena Tulli

was designed by David Bullen Design and printed at

The Stinehour Press in Lunenburg, Vermont.

The paper is 60lb Mohawk Vellum.

The text typeface is Dante.